Western
Bo
1993

Bowers, Terrell L.
    The secret of Snake Canyon / Terrell
L. Bowers. -- New York : Walker, 1993.
    155 p. ; 22 cm.
    ISBN 0-8027-1264-9

1. Western stories.   I. Title

InKo   18 MAR 94   27682103   IKPAsl   93-9756r93

THE SECRET OF SNAKE CANYON

THE SECRET OF SNAKE CANYON

Terrell L. Bowers

Walker and Company
New York

A c. 1

First published in the United States of America in 1993 by
Walker Publishing Company, Inc.

Published simultaneously in Canada by Thomas Allen & Son Canada,
Limited, Markham, Ontario

Library of Congress Cataloging-in-Publication Data
Bowers, Terrell L.
The secret of Snake Canyon / Terrell L. Bowers.
p. cm.
ISBN 0-8027-1264-9
I. Title.
PS3552.087324S4   1993
813'.54—dc20   93-9756
CIP

Printed in the United States of America

2   4   6   8   10   9   7   5   3   1

AUTHOR'S NOTE

CHINESE IMMIGRANTS BEGAN arriving in significant numbers in California during the gold rush of 1849. Even after slavery was abolished with the end of the Civil War, the Chinese continued to be indentured or under contract for up to three years after passage to the United States. Most of the men came to earn their fortunes and return to China.

It was forbidden for female Chinese to enter U.S. ports, so they were smuggled in, disguised as boys. These women usually were forced into at least three years of service in a joy house before they were free to seek a husband. Women were bought and sold and often fought over by rival tongs.

As more Chinese entered the country and settled in the Old West, they became a target of growing intolerance. There were riots against the Chinese in many towns across the country, as whites resented their industriousness and their willingness to work cheaply under the poorest of conditions. The Chinese were blamed for the silver crash, the recession, and for the loss of jobs. In the Land of the Free, the Chinese had no rights, no allies, and their only protection was to belong to a tong.

THE SECRET OF
SNAKE CANYON

CHAPTER 1

THE AUGUST SUN burned mercilessly on the flatland desert; its brilliant glare reflected up from the parched soil, forming an ocean of heat waves. Distant objects seemed distorted and unreal, blurred images above the burning plane.

Reese Corbett rode slowly and squinted against the relentless haze, trying to pick out any movement. A quick sweep of the horizon showed the only thing stirring in the furnacelike heat was a solitary hawk. High overhead it soared lazily, searching for unwary prey below.

With the tenacity of a bloodhound, Reese studied the marks on the trail. He was of singular purpose, on the track of two ruthless killers. It was bad enough to rob a bank and ruin people's lives financially, but these two bandits had shot everyone in sight.

Razor Back Jeeters and the Albino Kid had hit the small border town of Silver Thorn with a mad-dog vengeance. Razor Back had emptied his gun into anyone on the streets, while the Albino set fire to the bank and rode down an elderly couple, en route to his own escape. They had left a trail of bloody bodies and devastation as if a tornado had unexpectedly roared through the town. Five people had been shot, a half dozen more injured, including an eight-year-old child. Two of the wounded had died and the child had lost a leg. In the process of getting away, Razor and the Kid had taken a woman bank teller hostage.

Reese knew little about the clerk, other than that she was the wife of one of the wounded men. The couple had worked together in the bank. Her husband would recover, but by now he might already be a widower.

1

Razor Back had earned a reputation as a wild man. Reese figured the man's wagon was only turning on three wheels, for he was without compassion or conscience. He boasted to have killed fifteen people, "not counting Mexicans, Indians, or Chinese." The Albino Kid was not much better, but was more likely to kill from ambush. He was wanted for murder in two territories and at least one other state. The two of them joining up together was like mixing fire and black powder.

With a slight tug of the reins, Reese held back his mount momentarily and scrutinized the faint scrapes and prints on the trail. He knew he was gaining steadily on the two killers. It appeared that in order to conserve their horses' stamina, they were being forced to walk their mounts. *If only I could gain a little more speed,* he thought.

As he felt his horse stumble, Reese drew back the reins. He swung his leg stiffly over the pommel and slid to the ground. Dancer, his palomino, had been going full-out for nearly three days. Alkali dust covered his golden hide, matting his silvery mane and tail. Usually proud and high-stepping, the animal's head was only inches off of the searing floor of the desert. There was a limit to Dancer's endurance, and it was not far off.

Reese rubbed the horse's nose and patted his neck. After a few words of encouragement, he began to lead Dancer behind him, walking across the vast expanse of wasteland. He guessed the high, jagged peaks visible in the distance to be the White Mountains, although they could have been about any other mountain range between Nevada and California. He had been following the bandits' trail for so long that he had lost track of any familiar landmarks.

The sun grilled the crusty ground underfoot and baked Reese from his toes up. Within minutes, his shirt was soaked with perspiration and the back of his neck already felt like a well-done steak. He bowed his shoulders against the infernal heat and kept up a steady pace. He knew that he could not continue much longer, but neither could the two men and their hostage. The tracks he followed were only hours old. He was confident that he would overtake the two killers before they could make the mountain range.

In Dancer's saddle boot was his .50-caliber Sharps rifle. With the weather clear and no air movement, he could knock those two from their saddles at a thousand yards. All he needed was to get close enough to . . .

Reese stopped so suddenly that his horse bumped right into him. As he stared through the illusionary heat waves, he perceived a dark form on the ground.

His heart pounded, making his temples throb. He shaded his eyes with his hat, but was unable to see the image clearly. Quickly, fearful of the worst, he swung up onto Dancer's back.

"Come on, boy!" he said to his game little palomino. "Give me what you can!"

Dancer responded gallantly, bounding forward into an easy lope. The distance was shortened with every stride, and Reese was relieved when a woman struggled to push herself up to a sitting position. As if she lacked the strength to manage that feat completely, she lifted a single hand and waved at him.

Dancer was heaving mightily as he pulled to a stop a few feet from the woman. Reese dropped the reins, jumped down, and removed his canteen.

The lady, who was in her mid to late thirties, appeared ready to cry with elation at being found. Her face was burned from the sun and her lips were cracked and chapped. She could not utter a sound, as her throat was too dry and her tongue too swollen.

Reese removed the cap from his canteen and guided it to her lips. "Easy now, ma'am," he told her gently. "Take a sip or two and let it settle. Gulp it down too quick and you might buckle in the middle."

She showed incredible restraint, taking three or four small sips. He grimaced, seeing that she had no foot gear. Her feet were blistered and bleeding.

"Where are your shoes?" he asked angrily. "Did they take them?"

The woman tried to form a word, then nodded her head.

"I'm dang sorry that it's taken me so long to catch up," Reese told her, watching her take another couple sips of water.

This time the woman cleared her throat. "Y-yes," she managed weakly, barely able to form the words through her dry, parched lips. "That . . . that madman, Jeeters. A few hours ago, he made me walk. When I couldn't go any farther, they took my shoes and left me. Jeeters said the worse condition I was in, the more it would slow you down."

Reese realized at once that it had done more than slow him down. He could not follow after them any longer. The woman had to be returned to safety immediately, and Dancer could not pack both of them. Jeeters was as smart as he was ruthless, Reese thought begrudgingly. He left the woman near crippled and alive, knowing it would stop him. If they had killed her, it wouldn't have gotten him off of their trail.

"My husband," the woman said anxiously, "is he all right? He was shot . . ."

"Your husband is waiting for you in Silver Thorn. The bullet took a piece of one rib, but it didn't do any permanent damage. He'll probably be up around before you, what with those blisters and such on your feet."

As tired and weak as the woman was, she was visibly relieved. "I—I've been so worried about him, so afraid that he would die, that I would never see him again."

"Reckon he has been suffering the same worries about you, ma'am."

"I prayed that someone would come." Her eyes filled with tears, the emotion choking her voice.

Reese was moved by her outburst. To cover his own emotions, he offered her another sip of water. She resolutely recouped her composure, then took notice that there was no other canteen or water pouch on Dancer.

"Is this all the water you have? If my memory serves, it is quite a way to civilization," she said, refusing to drink.

"Yes, ma'am," he admitted. "We are close to two days from the nearest way station. By the time we arrive, we'll be as dry as the dust in a mummy's tomb."

She smiled at his remark. "Who are you?"

"Name's Reese Corbett, ma'am. I'm a deputy marshal out of Sacramento."

"Sacramento? Then what are you doing here, Mr. Corbett?"

"It just happened that I was on my way to Virginia City on business when I rode into Silver Thorn a couple hours after the robbery."

She took his hand between her own and kissed it gently. Then she smiled weakly and said, "I can never thank you enough for coming after me. If they hadn't seen you following and been afraid of you catching them, they would have certainly killed me."

Embarrassed, Reese put the lid on the canteen and returned it to the horse. He took a few minutes to dab some liniment on the woman's feet and wrap them in bandages. As she could not even stand under her own power, he put an arm under her and lifted her up.

"We need to get out of this hot sun," he said stiffly. "Dancer will enjoy having a lightweight like you on his back."

"But you can't walk all the way back."

"I'm not in my bare feet, ma'am," he replied, setting her into the saddle. "Besides that, we are rather limited in our choices."

"You are very gallant, Mr. Corbett."

"Yeah" was his only reply. Then he took Dancer's reins and started walking back across the expanse of desert. It was going to be a grueling trip back to Silver Thorn.

"There's a word for men like you, Corbett," Marshal Skip Davies told Reese firmly. "The word is impetuous. You don't stop to look how deep the water is or how wide the river, you just jump right in and start swimming."

"They had no lawman handy in Silver Thorn, Skip," Reese said, pleading his case. "I was the best bet to catch up with Razor Back and the Albino."

"But you came away empty-handed."

"I doubt that Mrs. Grey would agree with you."

He grunted. "Okay, okay, I know the story, Corbett. They used her to buy time for their escape." The give in his words was not evident in his posture. He had both hands on his hips, scolding Reese as if he were a disobedient son. "But if you had made the effort to round up a posse, there would have been someone else with you to have tended to the woman."

"Nine times out of ten, a posse slows down the pursuit, Skip. I work better alone."

"See?" he shouted. "That's what I mean—you are always too blasted impetuous!"

"I still got to Virginia City in time to give testimony. The Calico Brothers were both hanged."

"I know," he grumbled, "but what about this bill for expenses? Five dollars for the stage?"

"My horse was played out. I had to leave him behind and take the stage."

"Five dollars for a measly fifty miles? The coach is getting so expensive that a man can't travel anymore." The marshal's mood was beginning to soften. "Any further word on those two killers?"

"Didn't hear anything on my way back," Reese replied.

"They'll probably bury themselves deep until their stolen money plays out."

"Hate for you to drop a robbery and double murder, but I need you to ride to San Francisco."

"What for?"

Skip picked up a stack of letters from his desk. "I can't read but one of these; the others are in Chinese. Kim Lee is the name of a Chinese gent who has brought in thousands of immigrants in the past ten years or so. He advances their passage and then hires them out under contract. He is repaid by the laborers and draws a healthy commission from the companies that hire the Chinese to work for them. If you recall, the Central Pacific track was mostly laid by those hardworking coolies."

"So what is Kim Lee writing to us about?"

"I have to take his word on what all of these scribbled letters are. He claims that these notes are from concerned Chinese families."

"Concerned about what?"

"How do you feel about coolies, Corbett?"

Reese shrugged. "I spent a few months supplying meat for the railroad. Never had cause to think much about the Cantonese laborers. They kept to themselves and never seemed to bother anyone. As I recall, the only time I ever seen them make a ruckus was during their gambling. They play a lot of that *fan-tan* game involving the use of coins. Never looked like much to me, but they'd get pretty excited, sometimes downright provoked if luck ran against them."

Skip rested his haunch on the corner of his desk. When he looked at Reese, the light of compassion shone in his face.

"There is a great deal of sentiment against the coolies these days. With the railroad cutting back, there are thousands of them out looking for work. A good many labor groups blame them for the unemployment in California, as they are willing to work longer hours and for less money than everyone else."

"Yeah, I've heard some of the complaints."

"As I remember, things have been going against them for a number of years. The first time I saw the racial hatred firsthand was at the San Francisco docks back in '67, when the Pacific Mail Steamship arrived. The new Chinese arrivals were greeted with name-calling and a hail of stones and eggs. Some had to cover up and run all the way to the Chinese district. That was around the same time that an Anti-Coolie Labor Association was put together.

"Then in '69, right after the Union Pacific and the Central Pacific met at Promontory Point, there was a celebration in San Francisco that ended up being a riot. The mob turned ugly and went into the Chinese district. They beat up a bunch of Chinese, robbed and wrecked a number of their stores, and destroyed several houses for meanness' sake."

Reese rubbed the stubble on his chin and remarked, "I was with the railroad over at Truckee earlier that same year when the locals from town drove about fifteen hundred Chinese up into the hills, refusing to let them enter town or hold down jobs. I had never given much thought about them being different until that episode."

"It has only gotten worse in the past three years," Skip said. "You remember the pandemonium that took place in San Francisco's Chinatown last year?"

Reese nodded his head solemnly. "Yeah. Eighteen or twenty Chinese killed, dozens more injured, and the attackers got off without a single man being held accountable."

"That isn't exactly what happened," Skip argued. "One hundred and fifty men were indicted by a grand jury, and six were found guilty."

"But they were all released on technicalities!"

"Yes, well, the bottom line is, there is a great deal of anger directed against the Chinese these days. Even Governor Newton Booth stands on a labor platform that is prejudiced against them. There is never any action taken against someone who robs or beats up the Chinese. They're fair game and expected to look out for themselves."

"So what are the letters about—complaints against the white population or individuals?"

"Actually neither, Corbett. These are requests for information about missing relatives. It seems that a number of men have been dropping from sight lately."

"Who's to say they're missing?" Reese wanted to know. "They arrive in this country under a contract that requires them to work a minimum of two years and they're scattered all over, most of them not speaking a word of English."

"These letters say different, according to Kim Lee," Skip insisted. "He claims that a large number of new arrivals have disappeared without a trace, sometimes entire groups at one time. I don't know what all is going on, but I'm dead set against some of what is taking place, Corbett. Did you know that there are girls being kidnapped and smuggled into the country from Hong Kong? They are sold either as wives or as whores in the local joy houses."

"I talked to a translator one time who told me the girls come into the country with contracts and they have to work in the brothels for three years. After that, they are free to select a husband."

"Those are the ones who come willingly," Skip agreed. "But there are many others who are shipped in and simply sold to the highest bidder. That means that we are sitting by and letting slavery take place—after the Emancipation Proclamation freed all men."

"What can we do about it? Those Orientals are like a separate society from the rest of the country."

"This letter is asking for our help, and I think we should try," Skip replied. "Lee is afraid that these men are being killed by some underground network that is out to rid the country of Chinese."

"What can we do?" Reese asked. "Shouldn't the governor or President Grant himself look into that kind of thing?"

"According to Lee's letter, there's a lot of money being put into some influential people's pockets to prevent any investigation."

"So what are we supposed to do?"

"We need more than a couple of letters and a few missing people to start making charges against anyone. We need hard facts, some inside information, and a witness or two. If there is someone dealing in large-scale slavery or engaged in the murder of Orientals, it's up to us to find out and put a stop to it."

"That's going to be one tough assignment, Skip. Chinese die every day in the mines or on the railroad. There have always been accidents. I was with the railroad when an avalanche killed about a dozen of them at once."

"No one's denying that working in mines or for the railroad is dangerous, and accidents are bound to happen. But the people Kim Lee speaks of are not reported dead or injured. They come into the country and then are never heard from again. That kind of thing is right spooky, Reese."

"How do I go about finding anything out? I can't very well pass myself off as a Chinese and go undercover."

"You'll have to go visit Kim Lee and see what direction that takes you. If you find anything to warrant a full-scale investigation, I'll personally visit the governor."

"You think I can find out anything on my own?"

Skip shrugged. "If anyone can, you're the impetuous fool to do it, Corbett. You aren't afraid to take a chance, or step on big, important toes, or wade into a fight."

"Yeah," Reese grumbled, "I'll probably go snooping around in Chinatown and never be heard from again."

"I know you'd rather scout the hills for Razor Back and the Albino, but someone has to look into this."

"One day, I'm going to take up raising palomino horses, Skip. This line of work is about as exasperating as trying to catch the wind in a sack. I hate to quit midstream on a pair of murdering scum like those two killers."

"We'll find them, Corbett. Those two outlaws will surface somewhere, and when they do, we'll get them. This here is something that won't wait."

"Without my speaking a word of their language, I'll be hard-pressed to get any solid leads. What do I do about that?"

"Kim Lee ought to be able to help."

Reese sighed in resignation. "All right, I guess I'm your man, Skip."

CHAPTER 2

THE HEAT FROM the stove was suffocating. Alley Cat took one of the heavy irons from the hotplate and carefully pressed the Sunday-best dress. Even using the thick cloth around the handle, the intense heat was enough to burn her fingers.

Setting the iron back on the heating tray, she held up the fancy piece of clothing and inspected it for wrinkles. Impulsively, she paused to try to picture herself in such a pretty dress. Using one hand to fit it against her shoulders and neck, she sought her reflection in the room's single windowpane, but the image was only a vague grayish blur. She looked downward, envious of the woman who wore such a garment.

It must be wonderful to be able to dress in such clothes. She pivoted to allow the flounce to swirl at her feet. The thread of a smile turned her lips upward. How exciting to be a beautiful young girl, sought after by handsome men, all of them eager to hold her hand or clamoring for the next dance.

She reflected upon the time she sneaked into the monthly barn dance held at the edge of the white part of town. It was so exciting, spying on the fancy-dressed women, the men in their best suits, listening to the different tempos of music. Her heart yearned to be a part of such merriment.

Feeling suddenly sad, she put a stop to such silly, romantic thoughts. She used a wooden rod to hang the dress neatly on the finished-work rack and paused to sip a few swallows of tepid water. She mopped her brow with a towel and paused momentarily to fan her face, trying to stir enough air to cool herself. Working in the back room was the equivalent of being confined in an oven.

"Cat!" Martha shouted at her. "There is a customer at the counter. Tend to the front for me!"

"Yes, ma'am," she replied, hurrying out of the back room.

The fresh air in the outer office was a relief, but the patron at the door dampened her enthusiasm at once. It was the Chinese lord, Hoy Quan. He was wealthy and head of his own tong. As was customary for him, he was gaudily attired in a long-tailed blue coat with gilt buttons, embroidered white waistcoat, dapper buff trousers, and varnished boots. He carried a gold-tipped cane and constantly toyed with a silver-lined fob, checking his fancy timepiece as often as if he were being paid for every minute of the day. His scarf pin was jewel-encrusted and the size of a silver dollar.

"Ah, Missy Alley Cat, you look vely good." He showed his best smile, revealing two gold teeth. "How you like go work for me today?"

Cat ducked her head, using her unkempt bangs to cover her face. She was glad that she had not washed her clothes that day. Whenever Quan came around, she attempted to look as dirty and wild as possible. "No, Mr. Quan. I am not ready."

He sauntered up to stand against the counter. She could feel his eyes roam over her licentiously, like so many dirty hands, violating her modesty.

"I teenk you ready," he said with some force. "You not forget debt of mother? You not forget you debt to Quan."

She clenched her teeth together hard. "I haven't forgotten."

"You owe Hoy Quan two years' service."

"So you've been telling me for the past few years."

"You sometimes look like boy, Missy Alley Cat. Quan

teenk you try hide girl under dirt and baggy clothes. Mebbe not want pay debt."

Cat continued to stand with her shoulders bowed and head ducked. She wished to look as young and unattractive as possible, but Nature often intervened to work against her.

"You be vely popular, Missy Alley Cat," he continued. "Roundee eyes and pale skin get much attention. I pay you good. You pay debt, then be free to marry anyone you choose."

She shook her head again. "I'm not ready yet."

A fleeting glance upward showed that he no longer smiled, and his eyes glinted with impatience. "I wait for you grow long time. Quan also pay to raise Alley Cat. You owe me much money."

Cat suffered an instant mixture of anger and shame. She could not even look such a sleazy sort in the eye. Rancor, humiliation, and incredible internal torment assailed her until she trembled from the effort to control her emotions.

"What do you want from me?"

"You have no life in these place," he said. "What there for you to do?"

"I earn my keep," she replied.

"Twelve-hour day, six day every week," he countered arrogantly. "And you money?" His voice rose an octave. "What is you money?"

"That doesn't matter!"

"I pay much more, Alley Cat. You make much money work for me. Pay back debt of mother and self. Joy girl work only eight-hour day, get much money, good time, no work Sunday."

She maintained her refusal in silence.

"What more good for half-Chinese, half-white girl?" He was indignant. "What else you do that pay back Quan?" He laughed cruelly. "Who want half-Chinese girl?"

Martha entered the room. She had obviously heard the last portion of the conversation. She threw a hard look at Cat and said, "You get back to your ironing! I'll see to the gentleman."

Cat hurried into the back room. She had been keeping the draw-curtain open, to allow in some air, but she quickly pulled it closed. She did not want to have to look at Quan, and she certainly did not want him looking at her.

Even as she paused, trying to slow the pounding of her heart, she was able to hear the two of them speaking.

"Hoy Quan grow tired to wait," he said to Martha.

Her voice was more hushed. "I keep telling you, Quan, it ain't my doing. Alley Cat is being stubborn. I work her harder than I ever worked anyone else, yet she don't give an inch."

Cat went through the room and out the back door. She often stood outside for a few minutes to catch her breath. The heat and long hours sometimes made her dizzy.

Sitting on a splintery wooden crate, she placed her elbows on her knees and propped her face between her hands.

"Dear God," she murmured. "What's the use? I'm a freak." She felt a sob threaten, but she would not allow it. Too often she had suffered tears of shame or pity. She did not think that it was right to dwell in self-pity, but there were times she could not help herself.

Closing her eyes, she could not recall any happiness or laughter in her entire life. Born an unwanted child of a joy-house girl, she had been passed around from one woman to the next. No one wanted the little half-breed around. She did not belong in the Chinese section of town, and none of the white population wanted anything to do with spawn of the yellow race.

She remembered searching through garbage for food, hiring herself out to whites to pull weeds or paint fences so she could eat. When she did chores she was not paid the same as the other children her age because she was half-Chinese. She was not worth as much, no matter how hard she worked.

That had not changed over the years. Quan kept track of her and eventually got her a job with Martha, who owed him money. Martha was shrewd and coldhearted, working Cat hard with very little pay because she knew that Cat had no better place to go.

Martha opened the door and Cat jumped to her feet. Several times she had been scolded for neglecting her work. She half expected a tongue lashing.

But Martha did not seem upset with her. Instead, she showed a stern expression.

"You should not be so rude to Hoy Quan," she began. "He is only looking out for your interest, Cat."

"Hoy Quan's interest is always for Hoy Quan," Cat argued. "I have never heard of him doing anything that helped anyone but himself."

"You have never given him a chance," Martha said with some patience. "He has a point about you being old enough to pay your debt to him. You would do very well as a joy-house girl."

Cat felt her temper rise. "I don't want to be a joy-house girl, Martha. I'm not a prostitute!"

Martha rubbed her hands together, as if trying to find the words she wanted. "They are well treated, have fine clothes, expensive jewelry, and beautiful rooms to themselves. There are so few females for the Chinese that they don't think less of a girl for being in such a profession."

"I am only half-Chinese," Cat reminded her. "I lived with several white families as a child and I attended the white church. I know what is thought about such women."

Martha grew impatient. "Stand up straight, Alley Cat."

Cat did as she was told. Martha had struck her more than once, with a quick open-palm hand, when not obeyed. Rather than risk getting slapped, she did as the woman told her.

"Put your hands behind your head."

Cat swallowed hard, but slowly followed orders. She was unable to hide her breasts in such a stance.

Martha laughed with contempt. "Not old enough! Look at you!" Even as Cat hurried to drop her arms, she knew her days were numbered in the laundry. "You have a mature build, Cat. You can't hide it from Quan forever."

"I'll find some other way to pay my debt."

"It's only for a couple years!" Martha continued to argue. "Why not get it over with?"

Cat gave her head a violent shake. "No!"

"I'll bet Quan would let you sign a contract and limit the amount of time you wished to serve. Think of the money you could put away! After a couple of years, you would have enough to buy your own business. You could do anything you wanted!"

"What about things that are important to me—virtue? Pride? Self-respect?"

"Those are white notions, Cat," Martha said irately. "You'll never be white, so why not use your Chinese heritage to better yourself?"

"I could never let strange men paw at me or—or worse," Cat said quietly.

Martha did not reply to her statement. She put her hands on her hips and glowered at her with hot, unrelenting eyes.

"Then you darn well better get back to work, Alley Cat. I don't pay you good money to slack off out here all day!"

Cat rushed past her, back to the hot irons and the long pressing board. She began to heat the wrinkles out of a shirt, totally immersed in her work. When Martha strode past, Cat did not so much as glance up.

★ ★ ★

Reese followed the servant into Kim Lee's huge house and paused in awe of the magnificent splendor. Velvety carpet, glass chandeliers, gilt-framed mirrors, oil paintings, lovely tapestries, and leather-upholstered chairs. The hallway beyond the entrance showed a winding oak staircase, covered with a plush carpet. To one side, he glimpsed a bedroom that was canopied with silk and lace. He stared dumbly as a girl attired in apricot silk jacket and bloomers came forward. She had a tray in her hands, with glasses of assorted drinks.

"Missa Lee come soom," she said, her accent very thick. "You like drink?"

He picked one that looked like wine. "Thank you, ma'am."

She ducked her head demurely and backed away several steps. A round-faced Chinese man then appeared, wearing a colorful gold and orange robe and red sash. Reese noticed he wore enough jewelry to start his own store.

"I am Kim Lee," he said articulately. "Can I be of service to you?"

"Name's Reese Corbett. I'm a deputy marshal from our Sacramento office."

A look of interest appeared on the man's face. "Yes, I received a cable from your superior only yesterday," he said. "Rest please," he invited, indicating a seat.

He spoke to the girl shortly in Chinese. She bowed to him and disappeared from the room. At seeing Reese follow her with his eyes, he showed a satisfied smile.

"Mi Tang is a singsong girl," he explained proudly. "Very rare in America."

"That's different from a joy girl, huh?"

He smiled again, this time at Reese's obvious ignorance. "The singsong girl is refined and proper, with a wit to tell stories and a voice to sing like the most beautiful of birds."

"Sounds like a nice gal to have around."

"Now to business." He was no longer smiling. "How do you feel toward the Chinese people, Mr. Corbett?"

Reese met his intense scrutiny with a relaxed response. "Same to me as any other race. I reckon your countrymen have been the whipping boys for bad times, but I personally have no reason to dislike Orientals."

He accepted that without comment. "I came to this country over twenty years ago, a lad with nothing to my name. From the time I arrived, however, I made the effort to gain a knowledge of your language and customs."

"You certainly mastered the language."

Kim Lee accepted the compliment graciously. "Most who come to this land are intent only on acquiring wealth and then returning home. I left nothing behind but memories and debt, so I made this country my home. As you can see, I have done quite well."

"This business of yours, does it still include your bringing in men for labor?"

"Not any longer. I believe the government will soon put a halt to that sort of thing. There are many who feel that there are too many Chinese in this country already. I have used my wealth to expand into many fields, Mr. Corbett. I own several businesses in the Chinese district, as well as two others in the main part of the city. I own tollhouses and a number of casinos all across the state. I no longer rely on the import of my countrymen to provide me with an income."

"So what is the problem?"

"As I have a certain position in the community, the Chinese look up to me and seek my advice in many matters. I am something of a diplomat, keeping peace between rival tongs, settling disputes, and advising new arrivals.

"It has come to my attention of late that a number of Chinese have arrived, in labor gangs, who have not been heard of again. I have a list of over fifty names, all of men who are missing." His features grew taut and showed genuine concern. "It stands to reason that for every name that is sent to me, there may be a dozen more who do not have relatives or friends who know to contact me."

Reese whistled softly. "You are talking several hundred men."

"That is possible," Lee agreed. "These missing men have been reported over the past six to eight months. Sometimes it is only one or two men and other times it is an entire gang."

"You mentioned that before. Labor gangs?"

"Many of the Chinese are organized into gangs of about twenty at a time, when they are contracted in Hong Kong. They travel as a group and usually hire out to one of three or four major companies. They end up working as field hands for the large farms, or working in mines or on the railroad."

"And you've discovered some entire gangs that have simply vanished?"

"Yes, without any idea of where they might have gone."

Reese nervously rubbed his jaw with the back of his hand. "Do you have any idea of where to start?"

"There is another businessman in this town, a Hoy Quan. He also has made a great deal of money on imported labor. I am certain that he has not given up the trade. He might have some information about some of these people."

"You haven't spoken to him, then?"

"He is from the province of Sinong, and I came from Sinwai. We were supporters of opposite Manchu governments and are natural enemies. He has organized his tongs and I have organized my own. We do not speak to each another."

"And he is still bringing in work gangs?"

"To my knowledge, it is still the bulk of his business."

"Then some of the labor gangs that have been disappearing are probably men that he has brought in?"

"That would be reasonable to assume," Lee answered. "I also have letters concerning others, men who have served out their indentures. It is because of those free workers dropping from sight that I contacted your people."

Reese perked up at that news. "Now you are getting somewhere, Lee. The ones who are indentured by contract have little rights in a court of law. They signed up for the trip over here, knowing that they would have to work off their debt first. However, the free Chinese ought to be protected by the law, same as anyone else."

"I'm sorry that I have no further information to give you, Mr. Corbett. My only evidence is the many letters I have received. I fear that even if someone knows something, the threat of certain tongs will make many people afraid to speak."

"Just what is a tong?"

"You might think of them as groups or organizations, Mr. Corbett. Just as you have the different labor parties, unions and such, we Chinese have our tongs. I suppose you could compare a tong to a small country, made up of administration, council of elders, and general members. We have, within our numbers, our army to defend the lives and rights of our members. I myself have organized nearly a dozen different tongs."

"You think there might be tongs mixed up in this?"

He again showed patient tolerance at Reese's ignorance. "Practically every Chinese who has lived here in the United States for any length of time is a member of one tong or another. Whoever is behind this—should they be Chinese—would have a powerful army of fighting tongs behind them."

"Those letters you sent us. Were all of the victims last seen or heard from in San Francisco?"

"I believe so."

"I'd like to talk to a few of the friends and relatives who have sent you letters, Mr. Lee. The problem is, I don't speak your language. How do you suggest I question your people?"

"That could be delicate," Lee said. "If there is a conspiracy going on, you might well be the target of a *boo how doy*, a hired killer. To be seen working with one of the known interpreters would be like carrying a sign on your back."

"I can't take time to learn your language, Lee."

He raised a single finger, as a thought occurred to him.

"There is one I know, a young worker of mixed blood. She speaks good English and her Chinese is passable. I think she would be of invaluable service to you. I have not spoken to her about such a position, but she is treated like the lowest of dogs by her employer. I do not doubt that she would eagerly accept another job offer."

"A girl?"

Lee smiled. "Who would suspect her? She is ostracized by the Chinese because she is half-white. The white race does not accept her because of her Chinese heritage. No one would think of her as working for the law."

Reese considered that. "It would be a good cover, working with a woman, but it might be dangerous for her."

"For a little bonus, I believe the young lady would accept the risks."

"I didn't bring a lot of money. I thought that . . ."

Lee reached into his robe pocket and withdrew a small sack. He tossed it effortlessly to Reese.

"Five hundred dollars in gold," he said simply. "You can return whatever you do not use."

"Whoa! I can't be taking money for—"

Lee held up his hand. "You will need money to buy information or silence, to hire people, or to buy animals and supplies. This is no bribe, it is a contribution to discovering the truth behind these disturbing letters. I am not paying you for your services, merely aiding in your investigation."

Reese pondered that aspect. The way Lee put it, he would owe him nothing, for the man was not indebting him in any way. It was true that it often took money to accomplish a task.

"All right, I'll accept this as expense money. However, I will turn in a voucher for the return of this payment. Once we get to the bottom of this, you will be repaid in full."

"A most satisfactory arrangement," Lee agreed.

"How much do you think I should offer this girl?"

"She works for two dollars a week now. Offer her ten and I would think that she would follow you to the ends of the earth."

"Where do I find her?"

"She works in one of Hoy Quan's laundries. His white manager, Martha Howard, is the operator. I think that even though she works for Quan, she hates Chinese with a passion. It would probably be wise to refrain from mentioning anything about your plan in front of her."

"Quan again," Reese repeated the name. "He speak English?"

"He has not mastered the language, but he does make himself understood."

"Maybe I'll visit him first, before I search out that gal at the laundry."

"The choice is yours."

"What's the name of the girl?"

"Alley Cat."

Reese raised his brows. "Alley Cat?"

"She has no other name. She is the offspring of a joy-house girl. As a child she was passed around for anyone to look after. When she was a bit older, she ended up in several white households, working for her keep. She reminded someone of an alley cat, running about wild, and the name sort of stayed with her. Hoy Quan caught her scrounging for food one time and put her to work in the laundry."

"What about her parents?"

"Impossible to know anything about her father, and her mother died of fever before the girl was old enough to walk. If her mother had not yet fulfilled her obligation to her owner, Alley Cat may still be required to repay that debt."

Reese set down his glass of wine, untasted. The young girl's sorry situation soured his taste. How could anyone expect an orphaned child to be responsible for her parent's financial obligations?

"Give me some directions to Quan's place and the laundry and I'll be on my way." Reese tucked the gold into his shirt and stood up. "Remember, this money will be paid back."

"Money is the least of my worries, Mr. Corbett. It should be the least concern to you as well. If the tongs associated with these missing men learn of your efforts, they might very well post a *chin hung* for all to read."

"A '*chin hung*,' huh?"

"That is a public notice of some kind, challenging an enemy to a fight, or offering a reward for someone's death." He showed his easy smile. "I believe the latter would be directed at you."

After getting directions, Reese shook Lee's hand and left the mansion. He had nothing but the suspicions of one man, and yet he felt an ominous foreboding. The hair bristled on the back of his neck, a sense of imminent danger.

There was no reason to doubt Kim Lee's story. He came across as sincere and compassionate toward the plight of his people. He might have mastered the English language, but he held to his own loyalties and was trying to look out for the welfare of his race.

But if hundreds of Chinese were missing, finding them was an immense undertaking for one deputy.

"Should have started that horse ranch," he muttered woefully. "What have I got myself into here? Tongs, killers, a price on my head?" He headed down the street toward Hoy Quan's house. "I think old Skip done courted you down a rose-garden path . . . into quicksand right up to your neck."

CHAPTER 3

CAT AWAKENED AND tried to turn over, but she was bound securely. Her right arm was numb from lying on top of it, and her wrists burned from the tight cords. There was a feeling of movement, but the sack over her head prevented her from knowing where she was or what had happened to her.

She remembered nothing except a brutal hand crushing a damp rag over her mouth. There had been a sweetish scent of something soaked into the cloth and she had lost consciousness.

Feminine moans next to her told her that she was not alone. Bouncing about on a wooden floor, she felt the jarring motion of a wagon bed. She deduced that the kidnappers had grabbed more than one girl. Their destination was unknown, but she had her own ideas as to the purpose.

Her heart sank, fear twisted knots inside of her, and she strained against the ropes that bound her. It was wasted effort.

Cat bumped another body. The sharp inhalation sounded as if it came from another girl.

"Is someone there?" she asked in English. When there was no answer, she tried again in Chinese.

"Yes," a soft voice came back. "I am Ming Toy."

"And I am Su Chow," came another.

Cat waited, but there were no others. After a moment, Ming Toy spoke up again. "Where are they taking us?"

"I think to a joy house," Su replied. "They have gotten so desperate that they are stealing us from one another."

"Why kidnap us when all it would take is an offer of more money and I'd go willingly," Ming responded.

"Maybe we are not being taken to a joy house. Maybe we are not supposed to know where they are taking us?"

"But why?" Cat asked.

"There are places that some people do not wish others to know about," Ming told her. "I have heard some of the patrons speak of the gold mines, where the miners are locked away the whole time they work. The men from one level do not know what those on another level are doing. It is for security."

"I don't care where they take us," Su put in, "so long as they pay us good. I am not going to work for nothing."

Cat was filled with terror. She wrenched her hands against the cords, but could not manage to get free. The bag over her head was stifling. She lashed out with her bound feet and tried to sit up.

"Stop it!" one of the girls complained. "You're kicking me!"

"I don't belong here!" she cried. "There has been a mistake!"

"Quiet down back there!" a gruff voice snarled. "I'll take a whip to you if you don't keep down the noise."

Unable to free herself, Cat ceased her struggles. She fought to keep hysteria from overtaking her. There had to be a way out of her predicament. She had to think, to reason.

Hoy Quan was decked out in a mandarin robe with a fur cape, horseshoe cuffs, and a wide, colorful silk belt. Trinkets of gold dangled from his wrists and neck, and no fewer than five rings adorned his pudgy fingers. He was a round man, both in face and body. There was a shrewd awareness in his eyes as he listened to Reese's information and spoke in all innocence.

"No, I not hear for any missee Chinese," he told him

pensively. "You say there be many letters from relatives and friends?"

"That's right."

He frowned. "That strange, Mr. Corbett. Is few of new Chinese what know how write own names. Mebbe this be big joke, mebbe a hoax. What you think?"

"I was hoping you could help, Mr. Quan," Reese answered. "But you say none of your labor gangs have come up missing?"

"Me no follow men, once they contracted," he said simply. "I get paid, I no check them again."

Reese did not want to get pushy, but he found it curious that Lee should have a dozen letters and Quan would have nary a one.

"I thought sponsors were paid over a number of months or years?"

Quan's head bobbed up and down. "Many time is so. For many years, sponsors live in China and money is pay back slowly. New men come now, pay in front by contractor and make all better for Quan."

"And you have not received a single letter or inquiry about missing relatives?"

"Always Quan asked to look for someone," he said. "No change since come here. I no get letter for whole missee crew."

"If you hear anything, I'd appreciate your sending word to the local police."

"Will do, Mr. Corbett. Quan always try help."

Reese thanked him and went out into the street. It still struck him odd that one importer would have so many more inquiries and complaints than another. It was made all the more puzzling by the fact that Lee was no longer actively bringing in workers. Why should everyone go to him, instead of asking Quan?

His next course of action was to round up the translator and contact some of the people who had written complaints. The laundry where the half-Chinese girl worked was only a couple blocks into the white district.

Hoy Quan stood at the window and watched the stranger. He did not like the idea of such a man asking questions.

"What did he want?" Ti Kong asked in Chinese, as he entered and stood at Quan's side.

"Follow him, Ti," Quan instructed the chief of his fighting tong. "I am curious as to what he will do next."

"You want him killed?"

"Not yet," he answered. "No need to cause any suspicion. Once he finds nothing, he will go away. The whites will not spend a great deal of time worrying about a few missing coolies."

"As you desire," Ti replied. "I'll keep watch on him."

Quan stood at the window until Corbett was out of sight, stealthily followed by Ti. He was an excellent man for the job.

Ah Gow entered the room and waited for Quan to turn from his vigil. Ah Gow was another trusted man in his employ.

"Did you see the visitor?" Quan asked.

"I watched him leave. What did he want?"

"Reese Corbett is looking into the disappearance of some Chinese workers. Our friend Kim Lee sent a complaint to the U.S. Marshal's office. Corbett is a deputy marshal."

Ah Gow looked concerned. "You think he'll find anything?"

"How can he find something that doesn't exist? There is no proof, no witnesses. He is a blind man in the desert."

"Lee has many eyes. His tongs are some of the largest in this country. Do you think he knows what we have been doing?"

"He can only guess," Quan replied. "They have nothing."

"Wyngate sent an order for another twenty men today. No ship is due for at least a week."

"Then Wyngate will have to wait."

"He will not be happy."

"The girls we are sending should help to ease his pain," Quan said, showing a narrow grin. "A joy house is what is needed to keep his men happy, and contented men work harder. Two girls is a start. We will maybe add another one or two later."

"Two?" Ah Gow frowned. "But we sent three girls."

A sudden flush of anger darkened Quan's face. "Not the one from the laundry! You did not send her too?"

Ah Gow paled noticeably. "Your orders were to grab her and any others we could find. We did what you said."

"But not her! I didn't mean for you to put her on the wagon!"

"I am sorry, Hoy Quan. I did not understand the orders."

Quan swore in English, then stormed about the room, hands locked at his back, trying to think.

"No one comes back from that place," Ah Gow tried to console him. "She cannot do us any harm."

"I had plans for that girl!" Quan said bitterly. "When dressed in fine silk, bathed in scented water, with her hair shining and clean, she would have been a rare jewel. Men would have paid dearly to gaze at her—both white and Chinese men."

"What can we do?" he asked meekly. "The wagon has been away for many hours. We could not possibly overtake it before it reaches the tollhouse. From there, they will travel by horse. If it is your wish, I will try and reach the tollhouse and bring her back."

Quan wasted no time making up his mind. "Yes, bring her back. Take any man who can ride a fast horse and go. I don't wish for Wyngate's filthy guards to touch her."

Ah Gow bowed. "I know of two who ride well. We will return her to you."

Reese entered the laundry and offered the middle-aged woman a smile of greeting. She reciprocated with a stern face and open suspicion in her eyes.

"We ain't buying nuthin today," she told him flatly, her wrinkled face drawn into a scowl.

He ignored her hostility, looking past her to the back room. He could see a Chinese boy pressing clothes, but no sign of any girl.

"You Martha Howard?" he asked.

"State your purpose," she shot back. "I ain't got no time for dilly-dallying around."

"Business that brisk?" He tried to put a dent in her wall of belligerence.

"Business stinks!" she snapped. "Ever since them there yella mongrels showed up, I don't earn enough to keep a dog."

He nodded, as if sympathetic. "Yeah, I got to admit that this is the only laundry I've seen in this part of town that isn't Chinese. You must do good work."

She grunted at his remark. "Only way to compete is to keep Chinese help."

"Is there a Mr. Howard?"

"Died of cholera some years back. This laundry is all we had, so it's all I got left. Even then, I had to borrow from one of them squinty-eyed pigtails to keep from losing the place. I ain't much more than a hired hand. I manage the place is about all."

"Is that right? Someone said that you had a girl working for you, one that was half-Chinese."

"So?"

He noticed she seemed more suspicious now, openly examining him, wary of his every word.

He leaned forward and whispered with mock lasciviousness, "Always wondered what a mix would look like. I've been told that there ain't but two or three mixed breeds in the whole state. I'd be willing to pay to see one, if you would be so good as to call her out."

Martha no longer made eye contact. In fact, his query appeared to have touched a sensitive nerve.

"She ain't working for me no more."

Reese groaned inwardly, but restrained himself and asked, "You wouldn't know where I could find her? I'd sure like to actually meet one of them sorts face-to-face."

"I told you, she don't work here no more. She quit yesterday."

Reese reached into his shirt and dug out a gold coin from the pouch. He thumbed the double eagle deftly between his fingers, slowly rolling it from one knuckle to the other. "Like I said, I sure would admire to meet that half-breed. Be worth twenty dollars, if you happened to know where I could find her."

Martha began to sweat visibly, staring hungrily at the gold coin. She rubbed the back of her hand along her moist brow, then pulled at a few strands of gray-streaked hair that were out of place.

"I don't know where she went exactly," she started. "You know how them Chinese are. No telling for sure."

Reese smiled disarmingly. "This now and another like it—if you can find out. You see . . ." He let the words hang, looking over his shoulder carefully. ". . . I'm looking for some special girls for a select kind of business establishment. It's a rather lucrative house that caters to well-to-do gentlemen with . . . shall we say, exotic tastes?"

He saw the glint in her eye and knew she understood. He continued, "Anyway, this place offers some Chinese girls and some white girls already. What my client is really looking for is a cross between the two."

Martha perked at that news. "Maybe I can help you there. I . . ." She lowered her voice and leaned closer at once. "I happen to know that Alley Cat was going to be working in one of those very places."

"You don't say?"

"Yes, and she left with a couple other joy girls. I believe they were going up into the high country, somewhere over near the Comstock Lode mine."

Reese set the coin on the counter and tipped his hat. "If I manage to locate her, I'll drop by with another of these." He hesitated, before leaving the shop. "You wouldn't know how much of a head start they have?"

The woman snatched up the coin, as if afraid he might grab it back. As he made no such effort, she said, "Left during the night. I'd guess you're six or eight hours behind them."

Reese hid the disgust he felt for the woman, while forcing a thank-you from his lips as he left the laundry.

The girl is gone. You ought to walk away from this chore, Reese. This is beginning to smell worse than a skunk's den. You're heading for nothing but bigger troubles.

He walked toward the distant livery stable, wondering if he was about to embark on a snipe hunt. He was not altogether certain that Kim Lee was telling all he knew. Reese automatically distrusted the pompous Hoy Quan, who claimed ignorance of the entire situation. And now he had to track down this Alley Cat before he could hope to find any answers to this puzzle.

The timing of the girl's departure troubled him considerably. Was it only a coincidence that the girl had left the very night before he called for her? If she was inclined to be a joy girl, why would she have worked in a sweatshop like the laundry at all?

He picked up his horse, still trying to decide if he was doing the smart thing in following Alley Cat. She might have grown tired of hard work and taken the easy route to earning money. If so, the expense money from Kim Lee should persuade her to leave the joy house and help Reese.

It also occurred to him that the girl might have left specifically to avoid speaking to him. It was possible that she knew something about the disappearances. Marshal Davies had sent word to Kim Lee of an impending investigation, but there was no telling how many others might have also seen that cable. The girl might have been whisked away in the night to prevent her from talking to the law.

"Can't answer the riddle if I don't ask the right person the question," he decided aloud. "I hope Dancer is ready for some hard traveling."

CHAPTER 4

REESE HAD CHOSEN not to take the main trail. It was probable that the joy-house girls would be moved by wagon. He considered taking a launch up around the bay, through the Carquinez Strait and the Sacramento Delta. A further journey up the Sacramento River would have put him in front of his prey. However, there was a chance he might miss the wagon, or they might turn off before they hit the main road between Sacramento and Virginia City. Once he lost them, it would be too late to backtrack and locate them.

He rode hard along the peninsula, skirting the twenty-seven-mile-long southern arm of the blue-gray bay. Once he was into the lower foothills and rolling country, he pushed forward until full dark.

It looked like a storm was brewing, so he had a cold camp, picketing Dancer in tall bunch grass. Then he took a few minutes to cut a ten-foot sapling and gather a number of nearby bushy hemlock branches. By wedging the pole between the base of a hill and the crotch of a tree, he was able to throw up a lean-to in thirty minutes. It began to sprinkle as Reese stretched out under the shingled-branch shelter. He lay in his blankets and hoped there was not a downpour. The lean-to protected him to a point, but he had not made the roof exceptionally water-tight.

The fresh, clean scent of the light rain filled his senses. He enjoyed the sensation, and his memory conjured up visions of his youth, of hunting and fishing with his father. He recalled the man teaching him to strip a piece of birch bark for a fire after everything was soaked from rain or snow. He smiled, thinking of his father's beaming pride when eleven-year-old Reese had downed his first deer.

Even as a boy, Reese had been one of the better shots in his small hometown. At sixteen, he had won a turkey shoot against the best marksmen in the country. He won that same contest four years running and it landed him a job with the railroad, providing meat for the non-Chinese workers.

His mother had died in childbirth while bringing his younger sister into the world. She had married at seventeen and moved to Los Angeles. His father had died a few months after Reese joined the railroad, killed by some hotheaded cowboy named Concho Royal, who had been spoiling for a fight.

It had been three years, but Reese still gritted his teeth hard enough that they ached from the pressure. Until that point in his life, he had never struck another man in anger, never pulled a gun to shoot at another person. Even when he crossed paths with Indians, he had never had to fire his gun at them. Before the death of his father, he had never felt the desire to harm another human being. But he had quit his job and set out after Concho, who turned out to be a tough, reckless killer with a price on his head.

Reese had met up with Skip Davies during his search and informed him that he was going to bring in his father's killer for trial. Skip had tried to dissuade him, thinking he would certainly get himself planted in a boneyard.

Reese closed his eyes, the face of the sneering Concho still burned into his memory. The outlaw voiced his contempt of Reese's father, bragging about the way he had gunned him down. Saying that Reese was going to have himself a "like father–like son" type of funeral, Concho drew on Reese. In his haste for speed, he missed his first and only shot.

The shock and surprise on the man's face still flashed in Reese's mind. His own draw had been instinctive, a matter of self-defense. But his aim had been as certain as in a turkey shoot. The bullet had been squarely placed, right through Concho's left shirt pocket.

Skip had arrived in time to witness the shooting. Within a week, Reese was a deputy marshal. After six weeks of training with Skip, he was out on his own. For the past two years, he had been on one hot trail after another. His ability with his fists and a rifle had cut down several desperadoes and put another dozen behind bars.

It should have given him a sense of satisfaction, but it did not. He had learned quickly that most lawmen were of the same mold: men who were bold, daring, and enjoyed the excitement and danger that came with the job. Reese wasn't like that. He was able to do the work, but he was not the sort of man who wanted nothing more in his life than to live on the outer edge of survival.

In each job assigned to him, Reese threw himself into his work with single-minded purpose. He was relentless, never wavering in his duty, but that was what it was, his duty. He was not satisfied to have earned a reputation as a bloodhound. He wanted a wife, a home, children playing and laughing within earshot. The memories of life with his father and sister made him yearn for a family of his own.

"One day, Reese," he said aloud. "One day, you'll find yourself a sweet little woman and settle down to raising and breaking purebred palominos. Don't go getting killed before you get a chance to fulfill those dreams."

At daylight, he awoke to find a cloudless sky and the ground only slightly damp. He was in the saddle minutes later and moving. As the primary road was made for wagon travel, it often navigated around the steep hills or rocky buttes. In such places, Reese made up time by cutting across the range of hills and taking a shorter route.

He was traveling a hogback ridge, skirting a secondary trail, when he noticed something odd taking place near the mouth of a shallow canyon.

He pulled up short, looking down from the crest of the knoll he had been riding. On the basin floor below, he caught sight of several men moving about. As he watched, four men scattered to either side of the main trail, all lying or crouching among the rocks.

Their horses were picketed some fifty yards away, down in a natural hollow. Approaching their position was a solitary rider, a big man in buckskin shirt and denim trousers. He wore a coonskin hat atop his head and carried a rifle in one hand, the butt jammed tightly against his hip, ready for instant use. The man appeared alert, looking all around, but he was riding directly toward an ambush.

Reese had no way of knowing what kind of game was unfolding, but the four men were dealing a deadly hand to the lone rider. He did not want to get involved in something that was none of his business, but neither was he about to let a man be dry-gulched right in front of his eyes.

Jerking his .50-caliber Sharps from its specially made sheath, he was quickly on the ground. He tied off Dancer and took up a position that gave him full view of the basin below. As the lone man rode nearer the trap, he was ready to intervene.

"Hold what you're doing down there!" he called out. "This is the Law!"

Instead of the men being confused or backing off, the four of them all opened fire—three at him and one toward the intended victim.

For all Reese knew, the four attackers could belong to a posse. They might have been trying to get the drop on a hired killer. On the other hand, they had shot at him when he called out that he was a lawman. That meant that everyone had put their money into the pot.

"Time to ante up," he said tightly, taking a careful aim.

Bullets screamed and ricocheted off the rocks around Reese. The men shooting up at him were at a great disadvantage—it was very hard to adjust for distance, shooting uphill. Reese kept his rifle steady, ignored the gunfire, and squeezed the trigger.

One man pitched over onto his face.

The rider in the coonskin cap was down from his horse, shooting from up the trail. He directed his attention to the three remaining attackers, blasting away with his rifle. He got one and Reese downed another. The last man firing tried to change positions to find a better location. The rifleman from up the road called his hand with a well-directed round, knocking him over backward.

The echo of gunfire dissipated into a graveyard quiet. The man from up the trail stood boldly out in the open, shading his eyes, staring up toward Reese.

"Come on down, mate!" he called. "Let us have a look-see at them there polecats!"

Reese returned his rifle to its boot and mounted up. By the time he made his way down the side of the mountain, the man in the coonskin cap had dragged the four bodies into a neat row. As he approached, he saw the big fellow spit a stream of tobacco juice onto one lifeless form in disgust.

" 'Tis low-life scum, they is," he growled. "Thought you'd dry-gulch Rusty McCune, did you? Well, I'm think-ing you'll be giving that a second thought, you back-shooting varmints!"

Reese rode up to within a few feet and swung down. The man was broad in the shoulders, barrel-chested, with legs and arms like tree stumps. He sported a bushy red-brown beard and dark, expressive eyebrows. He must have stood six-foot-five and probably weighed about the same as a medium-sized grizzly bear. He showed Reese a mountain-man kind of grin, all his teeth showing.

"By all the saints, I'm glad we cut trails, sonny!" he boomed in a thunderous voice. "You saved me hide, 'tis no doubt."

"Why were they fixing to ambush you?"

He snorted with contempt. "It be plain as the nose on your face, mate. Ain't no four men alive what would try and take on Rusty McCune in a fair fight, 'tis the truth!"

Reese smiled inwardly at the man's odd use of Irish and American slang. He walked around the bodies and made a quick inspection of each. The gunfire had been short, swift, and deadly. All four ambushers were exchanging views with the devil by that time.

"You know them?" Reese asked.

Rusty jabbed the one nearest him with the toe of his boot. "'Tis a snake you see before you, this one," he replied. "He has done a bit of work up at the Grayson Tollhouse. 'Twould seem no surprise that the trusting Grayson has been robbed three straight times. This varmint has been scurrying out to squeak the information like a wee cornered rat."

"Well, name's Reese Corbett. I'm a deputy marshal."

Rusty stepped past the bodies and took his hand in a firm, bone-jarring shake.

"Mighty glad to know you, I am, sonny. Were you invited to the party, you could not have arrived at a better time." He puffed up somewhat. "Not to say that I couldn't have handled them on me own, but I still welcome your help."

Reese rubbed the fresh stubble on his chin. "Hate to spend the time to take these four back to town. I've got an important errand to run."

"This episode be nothing to sweat over, sonny," Rusty told him, waving his hand in a nonchalant gesture. "We'll drop the four of them in a hole and be on our way in fifteen minutes."

"The death of these men ought to be reported."

Rusty narrowed his gaze. "Aye, sonny, but you done said you were a marshal. Does that not make anything we do official enough?"

"But I need names, identification or the like. How will I—"

"A ferret and three rats is all they were, sonny. Ain't no one going to miss the likes of them. If it will set your mind to ease, I'll tell me story to the police, once I arrive in San Francisco."

"Well, that isn't exactly the normal routine, but—"

" 'Tis settled," he said with some authority. "Let it not be said that Rusty McCune held you back from whatever mission you might be on."

"Did I hear you say that these boys were robbing the tollhouse shipments?"

He jerked his head toward his horse. "Aye. They knew I was carrying a pixie pile of cash. There in me saddlebags, I've got near twenty thousand dollars."

Reese felt his mouth drop open. "You have that much money—with no one else to help guard it?"

Rusty turned his head and spat another stream of tobacco juice. "That much 'tis nothing but slag in these parts, sonny. The last shipment on the stage was four times that."

"Then why not send it by stage?"

"I'm for thinking the twenty-percent commission for guards and protection has something to do with it." He scoffed at the thought. "Bless the saints, I'm taking this to the bank in Frisco for a measly five hundred dollars."

"You don't look like a hired courier."

" 'Tis not a courier I am." He was practically indignant. " 'Tis delivering money to the bank, I am."

"Yes, so you are—"

"Grab something to dig with," Rusty said, cutting him off. "We'll not be wanting to be shoveling all day."

Reese removed what papers and money the four men had on them. He made a short list of items to be given to the next of kin, should there be any found. Then he and Rusty buried the men in a shallow grave.

"Where you heading, sonny?" Rusty asked.

"There is supposed to be a tollhouse up by the Comstock mine."

" 'Tis true, and that be Grayson's place. His tollhouse is maybe fifty miles this way from the Comstock. You might be a-knowing that you got to pay to get through Granite Gap."

Reese had been hoping there was only one tollhouse nearby. With two, he might guess the wrong one and miss finding the girl.

"Give me a hint, what be it that you're a-looking for, sonny?"

In spite of how shaggy and coarse the huge bruiser appeared, Reese instinctively trusted him. There was an honesty in the man's manner that went beyond looks. "Have you heard about either of them putting in a joy house?"

He guffawed at that. " 'Tis a-laughing I am. I'm betting you heard the story about that new joint, a way up yonder off of the Snake Canyon range. I've been for thinking old Mike was giving me the horselaugh about that."

"What have you heard?"

"Me mate, Mike, he done told me that he heard of some of those dainty-feet ladies being shipped up to the Snake for entertaining the nearby miners. I didn't give it much credit."

"Dainty feet—meaning Chinese?"

"Aye, sonny. You know that them yellow-skinned people wrap their girl children's feet when they are about five years old?" He appeared completely perplexed at the notion. "Bind them up so tight that the little tykes cry at nights, just so's they can have small feet. Be that odd or what?"

"Different customs for different people, I suppose. Look at the lace-up corsets our women wear to give them a more shapely figure."

He grunted. "Me, I likes a woman what has some meat on her bones. Got to be soft to the touch and a-plenty to hug and squeeze."

"So there's a new place being built up along the Snake Canyon," Reese got back to his business. "Know anything else about it?"

"Tough place," he replied. "I mean, we're speaking of men who chew railroad spikes instead of toothpicks, sonny. You go up there, you keep your six-shooter handy and your back to the wall."

"I didn't know of any mining back in that stretch of mountains. I always thought it was impossible to do any digging along the Snake's treacherous cliffs and steep-walled gorges."

"Mining ain't the question," Rusty said with some authority. " 'Tis the shipping of ore. Ain't nary a smelter for a hundred miles. The trail winds around more'n a snake going through a cactus patch. Clings to the edge of the cliff for half a mile or more, too. Take the luck of the leprechaun to haul any gold outa there."

"Then you've ridden the trail before?"

"Me destiny followed that road one time, but after treading that narrow path with a dozen pack animals, I was not of a mind to make a second trip."

"How did they ever get a camp built?"

"They had to cut and erect the house with nearby timber. What was shipped to them went in by pack-train burros. Word has it they have started a road toward Grayson's side of the gap."

"I'm obliged to you for the information, Rusty."

"Think nothing of it, sonny," he said with a grin. "Anything you want or need, call on Rusty McCune. When there's a hard job, I does it with me left hand. If the job is beyond the ability of ordinary men, I do it with me right hand." His grin grew wider. "When the chore is impossible, I use both hands."

Reese stuck out his hand. "I'll be seeing you, Rusty."

The man took Reese's hand in an almost overpowering grip.

"I'll be in touch, sonny," he vowed. "Rusty McCune is not one to shirk from his debts. Being that I owe you my life, and half of what I get for the four horses and tack of these here gents, I'll be expecting to pay you back one day soon."

Rather than argue, Reese withdrew his sore right hand and arm. "Take care, Rusty."

"Aye, and you do the same, sonny," the man called. "Watch your back up there at Snake Canyon."

Reese put Dancer into an easy gait, still smiling to himself about the big man he had left behind. Rusty McCune spoke like a braggart, but there was a difference between him and most other men who boasted. Reese figured that Rusty could probably do exactly what he claimed!

CHAPTER 5

CAT WAS WITH the other two girls, but the ugly brute, Mock Doy, paid them no attention. He shoved Cat into the wall hard enough to rattle her teeth and grabbed hold of her hair. She stifled the cry that rose to her lips, as he jerked her up onto her toes.

"Half-white," he hissed in Chinese, as if the words were vile and dirty. "You listen to me!"

She strained to be as tall as she could, trying to lessen the pull on her hair. She was repulsed at the nearness of the man. His repugnant breath was in her face, and his body and clothes were unclean from weeks without washing. He had tattoos on both bare arms and a scar that ran from his temple to his jaw.

"I tell you this here and now," he said, continuing to punish her with his cruel grip. "If you speak one word of English or give me any trouble, I will slice off both of your ears and your nose." His hand dipped down and returned with a gleaming blade. He held it an inch from her face, glowering at her with a malevolent scowl.

Cat sucked in her breath, too frightened to scream. Her pulse raced violently, as if the blood were trying to escape her body. Fear expanded the inside of her chest, while imploding her heart, as if crushed under the man's heel. Terror froze the image of the dagger into her mind. She could see and think of nothing but the wicked-looking knife. Horrified that he would cut her, she trembled uncontrollably.

"Do not doubt that I will use this," he threatened again. "You will look like a peeled onion if you refuse to obey me."

She stared with wide, mesmerized eyes, unable to look away. The razor-sharp knife glinted in the flicker of the lamplight. The slightest bit of provocation might cause the vicious man to fulfill his threat.

"You are headed to a joy house, Alley Cat. One man more or less will make no difference to you. As for me, I can make a nice profit off you girls for the one night we spend here at the Grayson Tollhouse. You spoil it for me and you won't have to worry about ever having a man want you again. Do I make myself understood?"

She barely managed to nod, as his hold on her hair had not relinquished a bit.

"Say it, half-white!" he hissed again.

"I . . . I will do as you say," she murmured in Chinese.

A satisfied smile on his face, Mock Doy released his hold. Cat was unable to breathe until he spun about and left the small storage room. Both of the other girls were there quickly to console her.

"Don't worry, little kitty," Su told her in a motherly tone. "It is not so bad to be with a man. Some are very nice."

Ming was quick to support her suggestion. "And if you show them that you enjoy their company, many will give you extra money that is yours to keep." She gave her a knowing smile. "It is hard at first, but when you have served your three years, you are free to pick a man for a husband. The money is very helpful, should you pick a man who is not yet wealthy."

"But I'm not indentured," she complained bitterly. "I should owe no debt for coming to this country. I was born here!"

Su sighed deeply. "I have heard Quan speak of you. Your mother owed a debt, and she died before it was paid back. Who else is to pay for her contract?"

"And did he not provide you with a job at the laundry?" Ming was quick to add. "You also owe him for that."

Cat realized that these two girls had no conception of

what it was to be truly free. They had been little better than slaves all of their lives. To them, being free was picking a man who suited them, after submitting to hundreds of men for money.

Soap, towels, and a pan of water were provided to the three of them. There were also three silk robes. They took turns washing, then powdered their faces with a little flour and passed around a bit of rouge to add color to their lips and cheeks. As they were to be presented to white men, their hair was combed out long and straight, rather than put into pigtails. Once attired in the silk robes, they were ready for Mock to have his auction of human flesh.

It was a nightmare in hell, the most wretched dream imaginable for Cat. The three of them were led out into a throng of cheering men, paraded through their ranks like prize trophies. The place smelled of whiskey, sweat, and cheap cigars. The acrid smoke hung over the crowd and burned her eyes. The three of them had to climb up a crudely formed stairway onto several tables that had been put together as a platform.

The men were boisterous and loud, shouting and cheering. Some even attempted to reach out and touch the three girls. Obstreperous laughter and vulgar remarks rang throughout the room.

Su and Ming were not shaken by the attention, but rather strutted about, smiling and actually encouraging the men to make more noise. Cat backed to the edge of the table, trying to get as far away as possible. She could only watch in fascinated horror at the antics of the two joyhouse girls.

Then a big man, wearing a suit and stovepipe hat, climbed onto a chair and raised his hands to quiet the crowd.

"All right, you men," he began, shouting them to silence. "I'm going to tell you straight off that we are going to have a few rules to this here auction."

There were some jeers and mocking boos from the group of onlookers. It seemed to Cat that every man in the room was staring at her with lecherous eyes, as if each wished to devour her a morsel at a time. She cringed in dread and apprehension, so full of fright that she felt sickness would overwhelm her. It took all of her strength to manage the combined tasks of standing and not losing the contents of her stomach.

"These pretty young flowers are only available for one night, so there sure ain't time for all of you to get to know them." He winked exaggeratedly and the men responded with a healthy round of laughter and cheers.

"So," he continued at length, "we are going to sell their company and a private room to three of you lucky men. High bidder for each gal gets to spend the night with her. The rest of you will just have to suffer and sob into your beer."

Again there was noisy laughter among the men. However, Cat noticed a distinct change come over the crowd. They were growing anxious, eager to bid and see if their money might buy the favors of a girl for the night.

The wagering began in earnest. In her worst nightmares Cat had never envisioned anything so degrading and disgraceful.

Su was first, and she minced about like a show horse in a parade. It was something of a competition between her and Ming to see who could bring the most money for her company.

Su's favors were finally bought by a burly yellow-haired man who spoke with a thick accent and was probably in his early fifties. She earned Mock a handsome fee of two hundred ninety dollars.

Ming was equally enthusiastic, actually pointing at certain men and encouraging them to bid on her. She toyed with the audience, teasing them, baiting them, laughing buoyantly, while flashing her almond eyes and swaying her hips. Her efforts were rewarded, for a skinny redheaded man finally paid out three hundred and sixty-five dollars for her companionship.

The man in the odd, high-topped hat took the money each time. Mock had watched the first two auctions from the floor, but he climbed up next to Cat for her turn.

"Remember what I said," he warned her, while displaying a false smile of friendship. His teeth were so separated that his mouth reminded her of a dull-yellow picket fence. His voice was laced with ice and his eyes glowed with menace. "You cooperate or you will have no ears and no nose!"

Cat was trembling; her legs were like two wilted flower stems, barely retaining the strength to hold her up. She was pushed forward until she stood only inches away from the howling, heated-up mob.

"This one is special," the auctioneer was saying. "She is half-Chinese and half-white."

Mock had one hand locked around her left arm, while he subtly twisted her right behind her back. The painful demonstration forced Cat to arch her back. The natural result was that her feminine attributes were more pronounced.

The auctioneer took a moment to point a finger at her. "Note the blue eyes, mostly hidden by her long bangs. And what about the fair white skin, the trim, but rounded curve of her figure. Yessir, this here is the pick of the litter. Who'll start the bidding?"

"Three hundred!" a man shouted eagerly.

"And fifty!" added a second.

It was as if every man in the room had suddenly decided to spend his life savings. Miners, freighters, hired hands, they all put in a bid. The frenzy eventually dwindled to a sour-looking Irishman and a dirty, unshaven Swede. It continued until they were up to more than four hundred dollars.

At last, the Irishman grew silent.

"I've got a high bid of four fifty-five," the auctioneer said. At the Irishman's nod of defeat, he began to finalize the sale. "That's going one time . . . going twice . . ."

"Five hundred," a mellow but firm voice came from the back of the room.

Cat's vision was blurred from the tears that filled her eyes, but she hesitantly located the new bidder. He was an unimposing gentleman, with a flat-crowned hat, black leather vest over a blue cotton shirt, and a gun tied a bit lower than most on his right hip.

"By gume," the Swede complained loudly. "Vhy do you vait so long to bid? I don' tink der man should oughta come here at der las' minute."

"The bidding is still open," the auctioneer told him. "I've got five hundred dollars! Are you in or out?"

The man snapped something in his native language and stormed out of the room. A pathway was opened through the crowd for the newcomer. Several spoke to him or patted him on the back as he passed.

"No English and no trouble!" Mock warned her harshly a final time. "You take care of your owner for the night and you keep your nose and ears!"

Quivering with trepidation, she went with Mock down the steps. The man who had purchased her for the night handed over a large number of gold coins to the auctioneer. Then he took her by the wrist. He was ushered through the noisy crowd by one of the bartenders. When they reached a small door, it was pushed open.

On shaky legs, Cat went with the man, a paralyzing apprehension tearing at her heart. She knew that she was going to suffer physical violation and that nothing in the world would save her.

The sleeping room had a single cot, one lamp, and a washpan sitting on a nightstand. The blankets did not look as if they had been cleaned in weeks or even months.

Reese closed the door and listened to the rowdy laughter from the other side. Crude jokes and remarks filtered through the thin walls for a time, then the crowd went back to drinking and gambling.

He experienced a mixture of sorrow and pity for the young woman. She was frozen with fear, standing as rigid as if she were sculpted in bronze. In an attempt to reassure her, he placed a hand on her shoulder.

The girl nearly collapsed under the weight of his hand, but quickly recovered. She ducked her head and pulled away. As he watched, she seemed to battle an inner war.

"I'm not going to hurt you," he told her gently.

She let out a deep sigh of resignation and submissively sat down on the edge of the bed. When she lifted her eyes to look up at him, tears wound tiny paths down either cheek.

"You can relax, Alley Cat." He offered her a compassionate smile.

She sat upright, obviously surprised that he knew her name. Blinking at her tears, she stared hard at him, completely dumbfounded.

"I know you understand and speak English," he said. "I need you to help me."

The girl studied him for a moment, then swept the room with wary circumspection. She still did not offer to reply.

Reese sighed patiently. "Don't be afraid of me. I won't touch you. I only paid the money to get you away from the others. You can trust me."

"M-Mock Doy," she whispered. "He said he would cut off my nose and ears if I spoke any English."

"You don't have to worry about his threats," Reese told her quietly. "If you'll help me, you won't ever have to worry about Mock Doy."

The girl's brow was drawn into a frown. "What are you talking about?"

"My name is Reese Corbett," he explained. "I'm a deputy U.S. marshal, and I'm working on an assignment that requires talking to a number of Chinese. Kim Lee informed me that you could speak both languages."

"Then you want me as an interpreter?"

"That's right."

She still appeared confused. "And you came all the way up here to rescue me for that purpose?"

"Why did they take you?" he reversed the question. "I presume you were kidnapped?"

"Yes. They say that my mother was indebted to one of the tong leaders. I am told that I must pay off that debt."

"Pretty flimsy excuse for kidnapping."

"The Chinese have their own laws, Mr. Corbett. You are risking your life to interfere with them. I am their property."

"People are not property."

"Chinese girls are," she argued stubbornly. "I am lower than the Chinese, for I am a freak."

He lifted an eyebrow, concerned that she sounded serious. "Who says that you're a freak?"

Her mood darkened visibly. "I'm of mixed blood and was born out of wedlock."

"I'm part Irish, part Welsh, and part English. Does that make me a freak, too?"

She did not speak, but slowly shook her head.

"So what is the difference?" he asked.

Her reply was simple and stated, as if there could be no doubt as to the veracity of such a conclusion. "You are not half-Chinese."

He did not intend to continue the argument with her. "Will you help me or not?"

"Mock Doy threatened to—"

"I told you," he said sharply, "I'll handle Mock Doy."

"He belongs to a fighting tong."

"The tongs don't mess with the white lawmen," he answered.

She was not convinced. "Maybe when you are in the city, with lots of other policemen. You are all alone."

"Give me an answer," he said, ignoring her reasoning. "I haven't got all night to debate the strength and terror of the tongs."

"I am deeply in your debt," she replied softly. "As you have purchased me for the night, I must do whatever you ask."

"We'll sit tight for a bit. It'll be some time before we can get out of here without causing a riot."

"Whatever you say, Mr. Corbett."

Reese walked over next to the door. He listened to the men out in the tavern, hoping that they would soon filter home for the night. Getting the girl out was going to be no easy task.

He had to grin inwardly, as a thought came to mind. *Wonder what Skip will think of my turning in an expense voucher for five hundred dollars to purchase a woman for one night?*

CHAPTER 6

REESE PACED THE cubicle, anxious to make good their escape, but forced to wait for the men to clear out of the tollhouse. Each time he looked at the girl, he experienced a twinge of pity.

She looked weary, insecure, timorous, not much more than a child even though her body was mature. On the rare occasion when she dared to lift her eyes or answer a question, it was painfully obvious that she feared for her life. She nervously wrung her hands, head ducked until her chin was nearly against her chest, shoulders sagging under the weight of apprehension. His efforts to speak to her seemed to give her little comfort. She was frightened, alone in the world, terrified of attempting an escape with a total stranger.

Finally the tavern portion of Grayson's Tollhouse was quiet. With no windows in their room, Reese was forced to try to sneak the girl out the main entrance. He opened the door a crack and peeked out cautiously. The interior of the large barroom was smoky, but deserted.

"All right," he said softly, motioning to the girl. "Let's get out of here."

Alley Cat obeyed at once. She kept close to his side.

Easing slowly out of their small room, he swept the darkened barroom with an all-inclusive gaze, searching for anyone lurking in the shadows or peering through a partially opened door. It appeared quiet, so they moved quickly, weaving between the tables, hurrying across the hard-packed dirt floor.

Into the night he led the girl, thinking that they had

made good their escape. But no sooner had the thought crossed his mind than a shout went up, a warning cry, the sound of an alarm.

Reese broke into a run, going around a shed and between several large rocks, then over a high mound of dirt. He slid to the bottom of a wash, with the girl right on his heels.

His horse jerked back against his lead rope and danced excitedly at their approach. Reese spoke softly and calmed him down. Cat's robe was too tight for her to ride astraddle, so he placed her up onto the horse sidesaddle and swung up behind her. She took hold of the pommel with one hand, while encircling his waist with the other.

The horse bolted into the night, dodging brush and trees, making its way toward the road. Low, sprawling branches reached out to slap and claw at them. Cat ducked her head against his chest to ward off the beating, but did not utter a sound. Reese lowered his own head and bulled through the stinging swat of the branches.

Once onto the main trail, Reese gave Dancer his head, letting him feel his way along the black, winding path. From back toward the tollhouse, the sounds of shouting men still reached his ears. Some would soon follow. Reese needed to get far enough along the road to find a break in the steep canyon walls. Once into the rocky terrain of the surrounding mountains, he would be able to lose the pursuit.

"If we can get into the hills by daylight, we'll circle and backtrack until we shake them."

"I am not worth the risk of your being hurt or killed," she told him quietly. "You are stealing property that does not belong to you. The tongs will not stand for that."

"I told you before," he said firmly, "you are not property."

She looked at him, and said, "All Chinese girls are

property until they are freed from their contracts. I owe for my mother's contract."

"That's a pile of horse dung!" he snapped. "People are free in this country. Besides that, you can't be held responsible for the woman who bore you."

"The debt she owed is mine," she insisted. "I have been told that I must honor that contract."

"You want me to take you back?" he asked impatiently.

She wilted at once. Her answer was barely audible and very childlike. "No."

"Then you better make up your mind to help me think of ways for us to keep out of their clutches."

Reese glimpsed something stretched across the road. Even before he could sound a warning, a length of rope hit them both about chest high and knocked them out of the saddle.

As he was on behind Alley Cat, he tried to catch the girl in his arms. The hard earth slammed against his back and head, jolting the wind from his lungs and any coherent thoughts from his mind.

Reese gasped for air and pushed the girl off him. He tried to get hold of his gun, but a Chinese face flashed in front of his eyes and something crashed down against his skull. The world was instantly a dark void, spinning violently, filled with an incredible pain that split his head in two pieces.

In the distance, he heard someone speaking Chinese. What limited thought patterns he could muster were confounded with disbelief. Mock Doy must have somehow figured he would try to steal the girl and had been waiting with a rope stretched across the road. The idea seemed inconceivable, but it was the only possible explanation.

The girl's voice protested about something and he heard her get slapped resoundingly for her trouble. Reese felt someone going through his pockets. His gun was lifted from its holster, then a tranquil blackness engulfed his consciousness.

The first moments of awareness brought Reese raw, searing agony. His arms felt as if they had been pulled from the sockets. Every breath was labored and sent new waves of pain through his entire body. He blinked against the rays of the morning light, trying to chase the cobwebs from his brain.

He realized he was dangling by his wrists, hanging from a tree. Surrounding him was a sea of angry faces.

"So the half-chink got away?" one of the men said, sneering at him. "You tried to keep her for yourself and she coldcocked you for your trouble."

Another grumbled. "This stupid clod let the gal escape. We'll never get her back now."

"She was a real beauty, too," added a third.

"Well, sir," one of the miners said, glaring at Reese. "You won't never get another chance to steal one of them joy girls. We're going to break every bone in your body and leave you for coyote bait!"

Reese worked air into his lungs and tried to form words. Before he could manage that herculean feat, a driving fist hit him flush in the stomach and the breath was driven from his lungs. His head felt as if someone were setting off explosive charges inside his skull. He gasped for air, but could not manage a word in his own defense.

"I done brung my bullwhip," a rough voice grated. "Stand back and give me room."

"Shred his hide!" encouraged one of the others.

"Teach the thief a lesson he won't soon forget!" cried another.

Reese had no feeling in his hands, his arms were on fire, and his lungs screamed for relief. Dangling helplessly, he had no chance to even explain. They were going to beat him to death.

The braided rawhide snaked through the air, whistling like the arrow from an Indian's bow. When it made contact with his skin, it was the taste of a streak of lightning.

Reese groaned, too weak and miserable to manage any other sound. The welt, left on his back and ribs, felt as if a white-hot branding iron had been used to draw a path on his flesh. He clenched his teeth, preparing for the next crack of the whip.

"By the saints! That'll be enough, boys!" a coarse, vaguely familiar voice cut the morning air.

"Now wait a minute, Rusty," someone protested. "You don't know what is . . ."

The sudden blast from a gun split the crowd, and a bullet kicked up dirt at the man's feet. He silenced his objections at once. Reese watched in agony, his eyes opened to tiny slits. He spotted Rusty McCune, gun in either hand, facing down the near-dozen miners.

"Me next bullet will go a wee bit higher," he warned. "Possibly through your well-rounded middle!"

"This here feller stole a girl from the tollhouse last night," the man explained hastily. "We were teaching him a lesson."

"You'll be cutting him down, I'm a-saying . . . right now!"

"What has gotten into you, Rusty?" one asked. "You taking sides with a no-good kidnapper?"

"Cut him down!" Rusty ordered a second time. "I'll not be a-saying it again."

Reese felt the ground under his feet, but he was too drained of strength to stand. He went down to his knees. The rope was removed from his wrists and he sagged to the ground.

"Where's his gear?"

"Everything else was gone," one man replied. "His horse, gun, and tack were all missing when we found him this morning. We figured the girl hit him over the head and robbed him of all he had."

Rusty spat a stream of tobacco juice into the dust. " 'Tis amazing to me that you bunch of boneheads can stand upright. I'm for thinking you don't share a brain betwixt you. Git on back to your holes or under your rocks, from whence you crawled out."

Grumbling and still arguing among themselves, the group of men broke up and began to leave. Rusty put away his guns and produced a canteen.

Reese took several swallows and tried to get some feeling back into his hands. His wrists were raw from the rope, his head felt as if it had been split open, and the welt on his back stung with each breath. Even so, it was not pain that Reese dwelled upon.

"Mighty glad to see you again, Rusty."

The big, hairy man grinned. "Looks like you need watching over, sonny. You almost ended up ready to be skinned like a side of venison."

"You made good time getting back."

"Soon as I delivered me package to the bank, I changed horses and come back without stopping for sleep." He laughed shortly. "Somehow, 'twas in me mind that you'd be needing help. I remembered you was heading for Grayson's Tollhouse, so I set out for here."

Reese told Rusty about Alley Cat, without going into details about the investigation. "I had the girl and got away clean—or so I thought," Reese said. "I can't imagine how that Chinese got here ahead of me."

But Rusty shook his shaggy head. " 'Tis mistaken you are there, sonny. Mock Doy was still at the tollhouse with the two girls raising a ruckus about one of his girls' being stolen last night. 'Twas he that told me about the men having just left. So I followed 'em."

"What?" Reese frowned while gently rubbing the bump on the side of his head. He blinked back the throbbing pain, trying to absorb that information. If Mock Doy didn't have Alley Cat, who did?

Rusty helped Reese onto his horse so they could ride double back to town. But first, Reese wanted to go over the area where he had lost the girl. Rusty dismounted and examined the tracks, checking several clues before returning to give Reese his conclusion.

"Whoever took the girl did not head back to Grayson's."

"Any idea where he went after he took the girl?"

"Back toward the city," he replied. "And there were at least two others besides the girl."

"Something sure don't fit here, Rusty. If my head wasn't broken into a dozen tiny pieces, I might start some serious contemplation about this whole deal."

"So what will you be wanting us to do until your brain gets unscrambled, sonny?"

He stared at the big man. "Us?"

"Aye," he replied. "I owe you for saving me life. I'll not be forgetting that."

"You saved my hide just now. I'd say that makes us even."

He laughed at that. "That was only a little teasing. 'Tis paying you back proper that I intend, sonny." He puffed up his chest. "Ain't no one ever said that Rusty McCune don't pay his debts in full. I'm a man of me word, and me word is as good as the richest gold ever taken out of this here state."

Reese did not argue further. "Whatever you say."

"Then we'd best be rounding you up another horse and gun."

"I'd appreciate your help, Rusty."

"Let's head back up to Grayson's Tollhouse. He always has some extra mounts for sale, and maybe we can pick you up a gun, too."

"You sure about going there? Those guys might—"

"Trust me, sonny," Rusty said, silencing his objections. "You'll get nothing but respect, so long as you're with Rusty McCune. I can whup any ten of them put together, and they all be knowing it."

Reese checked his pockets. "Those Chinese took my money, except for this pouch inside my shirt. I've got . . ."

"Don't be worrying money," Rusty insisted. "I made a sale of those four nags and saddles that those bandits were riding. Half of that money belongs to you. It'll be plenty to purchase another horse and tack."

"All right, my friend. You're calling the square dance, so I'll play along with your tune. Let's get going."

CHAPTER 7

CAT WAS IMPRISONED in a small, windowless room. There was nothing in it but a blanket on the floor and a pitcher of water. She wore the same green silk robe and shoes as when she was abducted from the deputy marshal.

A thousand times, her mind went over the events that had taken place. Why did Quan's men bring her back to the city instead of turning her over to Mock Doy to go on to the faraway joy house? Whatever their motives, she was relieved that Mock Doy had not put in an appearance, for she was afraid he would have kept his promise and used a knife on her.

A heavy burden of guilt weighed on her shoulders at the events that had taken place. Reese Corbett had been clubbed unconscious, and he might even be dead. She bit her lower lip. Reese had been like a shining knight from a fairy tale, telling her that she had worth, that she would be free of any debt to Quan. More than that, she had been ready to believe him.

Cat wrestled with the torment of her emotions. She feared for her own life, what terror might lie in store for her. Yet she still worried about the stranger. Did he escape? Was he still hurt and bleeding?

The door opened without warning. She froze, staring at the woman who framed herself in the opening. Elderly, with thick powder covering her face, hair done in American fashion, eyes shadowed with blue paint and her lips as red as ripe strawberries, she looked like a porcelain doll. Her dress was yellow silk, trimmed with gold lace. Without having ever seen one, Cat knew this was a turtle woman, a Chinese madam.

"You can make it easy or hard on yourself, Alley Cat," she said in Chinese. "Resist and you will be punished. Comply and you will be well treated."

"What do you want from me?" she asked.

A slender smile curled the woman's full lips. "You are not so innocent to ask such a question."

Cat suffered a renewed pounding of her heart. "I don't wish to be a joy girl."

The smile faded at once. "You are in no position to dictate what you want or do not want," she stated firmly. "However, you are fortunate to have an option."

"What kind of option?"

"Hoy Quan has taken some interest in you. If you should consent to please him, serve in his house, you would be spared the duties of a joy-house girl."

Cat thought of the sallow-faced man, recalling his leering eyes and lurid suggestions. To serve him was unthinkable.

"You need not make up your mind this minute," the turtle woman said. "Take some time and consider your fate."

"How long am I to be kept a prisoner?"

"You owe two years of service to Quan. Part of that debt, I'm informed, is carried forth from your mother. The rest is what you owe him for his seeing to your care over the past few years."

Cat shook her head. "I don't owe him for taking care of me. I have always earned my keep. No one ever gave me anything. As for my mother, she died because of the life she had here in America. What more does Quan expect for payment than a person's life?"

"I only know what I was told."

"Yes," Cat said with some strength. "And I can imagine who told you such things. You're part of a kidnapping. There is a law against that in this country!"

The woman laughed at her as if the idea were ridiculous.

"Chinese girls are stolen back and forth by different tongs all the time. You are not a white woman, Alley Cat. You are Chinese. You have no rights."

"I am an American citizen," she argued. "I was born here and my father was an American."

"Who knows what your father was." The woman's voice turned cruel. "You are the offspring of an unknown night visitor. But your mother was Chinese. Regardless of where you were born or who your father was, you are Chinese, Alley Cat. If anything, you are a mongrel, a little alley cat who does not fit into either society." She glared hard at her. "I should think that you would be very happy that a powerful man like Hoy Quan should show an interest in you at all!"

The woman's words echoed Cat's own self-doubts. Never in her life had anyone treated her like an equal, neither the Chinese nor the Americans.

When Cat did not debate further, the turtle woman accepted victory and her tone again changed. "If you remain in my service, you will be called White Lotus. You will have a room of your own, scented baths, nice clothes, jewelry, and fine oils and perfumes. The working day does not begin until late afternoon and there is no working at all on Sunday." She let the words hang in the air. "Think about it, White Lotus."

The door closed, leaving Cat in the dark interior, alone with her doubts, fears, and apprehensions. Her fate was sealed. Either she would become White Lotus and serve several men each night, or she would end up serving Hoy Quan.

"Dear God, what am I to do?" she murmured her prayer softly. "How I wish You had watched over Reese Corbett. He"—she swallowed a constriction that rose in her throat—"he said that I was—was as good as anyone else. I would really like to believe that, if only . . ." She could not continue; her heart was too full of sorrow. She cried for herself, for Reese, for what lay ahead.

Kim Lee listened to Reese recount how he lost the girl. He did not interrupt, but showed an instant understanding of the situation.

"Is it possible you were being followed from the onset, Mr. Corbett?"

"Why should anyone be on my trail?"

"Word has undoubtedly spread about you being a deputy marshal. Word travels much quicker than a horse or carriage in our part of town."

"I only started to look for a translator," Reese said. "How much could have been learned before I even started to talk to people?"

"Perhaps they saw you come to me. I am considered something of a troublemaker among certain circles. My tongs are often involved in helping the oppressed of our honorable circle of members. It is no secret that I have been searching for answers into the disappearance of so many of my people. The cables coming into this part of town pass before many eyes."

"Since when would a Chinese attack a white man, mate?" Rusty spoke for the first time.

Lee nodded in agreement. "We have our *boo how doy*, our hired killers. They are trained to fight with all manner of weapons and are very deadly. However, they would never attack a white man, except upon strict orders from the tong leader. I believe they hoped that the darkness would prevent you from recognizing any of them as being Chinese."

"So where would this tong have taken the girl?" Rusty demanded. "I'm thinking that time is not on our side!"

Kim Lee did some pondering on that question. After a brief pause, he held up a single finger. "If Alley Cat was brought back to Chinatown, they would want her buried deep from any questions or searchers."

"So?"

"Possibly they would keep her in one of the many hiding places within the casinos or joy houses. There are secret passages, trapdoors, and the like all through those places. They use them anytime there is a raid by the vigilante police."

"I figured the San Francisco police were mostly bought off?" Reese said.

"That is true enough, but they still must go through the motions. There are some missions, near the Chinese districts, that seek out the slave girls. When they can free them, they will take them in and care for them until the girl finds a husband. That usually does not take long, with several hundred Chinese men to every woman."

"You'll pardon me for saying so, but that is little help, mate," Rusty said. "There be a great many of those joy houses around. 'Twould be like looking for a cricket in a cornfield."

But Lee pointed a finger at his own temple and tapped the side of his head. "Even within a cornfield, the crow knows how to catch the cricket." He smiled at Rusty's frown. "I happen to know of one particular house that would be a good starting point. Hoy Quan owns the place, and the man you mentioned, Mock Doy, is often seen there. It is likely that his men were involved in capturing Alley Cat. If so, it's possible that he would want her taken to that place."

"What's the name of that house?"

"The Love Garden, several blocks into the central part of town. The girls there all have names of different flowers: Yellow Rose, Lilac, Sunflower, and the like. To my knowledge, it is the only joy house owned by Hoy Quan."

Reese narrowed his gaze at the mention of him. "You

keep tossing that gent's name around, Lee. Do you know more than you are telling me?"

"I have no proof of anything, Mr. Corbett," he said simply. "I mention the fact only because you are familiar with the man. You did go to speak to him, did you not?"

"Yes. He was helpful enough, but claimed to know nothing about any missing people."

"That is probably the truth of the matter, then."

Reese was unable to detect any suspicion or malice within Lee's comments, but there was something there. Reese sensed that Lee had a genuine dislike for Quan. Whether it was because they came from rival provinces or for some other reason was something he wished he knew.

"I will have some of my more trusted people snoop around, Mr. Corbett, in case you fail to locate the girl. It is only a matter of time before we find her." He paused. "I can only wonder if she knows something of importance. Why else would they take her away from you?"

"I don't know, Lee. First, she was taken from the laundry. Then, when I rescued her during the night, someone snatched her away again."

"It makes one wonder if once you get her back, she will have any use as an inconspicuous interpreter."

Reese replied, "I guess that depends on who's got her and why."

Lee nodded. "If there is anything else I can do, feel free to call on me."

No sooner had they reached the street than Rusty shook his shaggy mane. "The man talks mighty fancy, does he not?"

"He does for a fact," Reese replied. "You, on the other hand, have the strangest mix of lingo I've ever run across."

Rusty chuckled. "Aye, 'tis an odd mix I am meself. Came from Ireland as a wee lad with me folks. At seventeen, I threw me lot in with a trapper. Between me native accent and me years of association with those mountain men, 'tis a rare mix of homespun blarney and backwoods wit I have."

"You said you knew of the joy house Lee mentioned?"

"Aye. I have seen that Love Garden once in passing. Do you want that we should mosey down there and take the place apart?"

"Let's try not to start a riot."

"To be sure," Rusty assured him. " 'Tis thinking I am that we'll only have to snoop around a little. Them Chinese madams don't usually want trouble."

CHAPTER 8

HOY QUAN STOOD at the window, listening to Ti Kong, his tong fighting chief. Ti had been following Corbett from the time he left Quan's until Corbett and his companion returned to town an hour ago. Ti had seen Ah Gow and the others steal Alley Cat and leave Corbett wounded, for the mob to find. Ti had watched unobserved as the big man with the guns saved Corbett from being killed.

"Who is this big man?" Quan asked.

"It is a puzzle. Corbett rescued the man from ambush, while on his way up to Grayson's Tollhouse. The two of them killed the four who were setting the trap. They were Wyngate's men."

Quan stared at the table and regarded Ti with a tight frown. "Wyngate's men?"

The man gave a solemn nod.

"What else?" Quan could not hide his anger.

"The two went in different directions, so I followed Corbett. The big man returned the following night in time to save Corbett from possibly being beaten to death. They travel together now. I think Tin Hau smiles upon that man."

Quan ignored his remark about the queen in heaven. "And now both men are in town?"

Ti nodded. "I stopped following them once they discovered Corbett's horse at the stable."

"What did he do about that?"

Ti grunted in contempt. "He paid the liveryman for his own horse and tack. The man is made up of twenty-dollar gold pieces."

"It was fortunate that you met up with Ah Gow and had them set a trap for the American. It is too bad the men from Grayson's place did not finish him off for us."

Quan went over to his desk and sat down. He took up his water pipe and toyed with it for a few minutes, deep in thought.

"What are your orders?" Ti was impatient.

"You did not say how this man wound up with Alley Cat in the first place. How did he take her from Mock Doy?"

"Ah Gow had just reached the tollhouse when I followed Corbett there.

"I only know what I saw from my place at the dirty window. Mock Doy was involved in an auction that night. He sold an evening's favor of all three girls at a bidding contest. Corbett purchased the night with Alley Cat. I then kept vigil and saw that Corbett was going to try and steal the girl. I rounded up Ah Gow and we prepared to catch them on the trail. After I gave the alarm at the tollhouse, he rode into our trap perfectly."

Quan was angered that Mock should be trying to work his own sideline operation. No one had given him permission to auction off the joy girls at the tollhouse. The man was growing too independent.

"What would you suspect our marshal will do now?"

"As he returned to the city, he must be looking for Alley Cat."

Quan slammed his fist down onto the top of the desk. "But why? What does she know?"

"She was with the other two girls," Ti offered. "Perhaps she learned of their destination."

"That information would do no good to anyone. Wyngate has made no secret that he is putting a road back to Gold Spur, at the head of Snake Canyon."

Ti shook his head. "Then I have no idea."

Quan squirmed in his chair. He wanted Alley Cat for his own, but not at the risk of fouling his deal with Lowell

Wyngate. He would have to think of business first and pleasure second.

"Our marshal friend might want to question Mock Doy," he decided. "Send Mock to see me as soon as he returns. This scheme of his to sell the joy girls for a night and keep the money secret is not the act of a loyal employee. I must decide what to do about that."

"I understand."

"Also," Quan continued. "If I were this marshal, I would want to speak to him, also. I would want to know everything he could tell me about the destination of those girls. We'll have to prevent that meeting from taking place."

"I will seek out Mock Doy," Ti promised. "What of the marshal?"

"Take Ah Gow over there and keep watch at the Love Garden. If Corbett shows up there, you are to do whatever is necessary to prevent him from getting Alley Cat back."

"To the point of killing the marshal?"

"We must do whatever it takes," he reiterated. "If death comes to Corbett, we can dispose of the body discreetly."

"It will be as you order."

"Go now," Quan ordered. "I want no mistakes."

"There will be no mistakes."

Quan watched him leave. His better judgment told him that he was taking irrational chances. He had ordered physical resistance against the lawman. That was a dangerous step to take. One mistake and he would have all of the Chinese-hating locals at his doorstep.

But he had to take chances. If he was ever to seize control of the Chinese district, he had to gather support and money enough to beat Kim Lee's fighting tongs. He would settle for nothing less than being the Manchu king of San Francisco.

Still, he suffered with apprehension, worried about taking on Reese Corbett. He was not a *Melican mandarin,* a crooked official of the law to be bought off. Killing him might bring in an army of marshals.

"He must know something!" Quan snapped aloud, going back to his water pipe. "And where does he get the money? Who is supporting his investigation?"

He suspected Kim Lee, who had the money to back an extensive inquiry into the disappearance of the many Chinese. He might even be charging people a finder's fee, money paid for his efforts to locate those missing people.

Quan ceased his worrisome contemplation, and a slight smile played along his lips as a thought occurred to him. Mock Doy had sold the girl, Alley Cat, for a single night. The fact that Corbett stole the girl from him was no secret. What would make more sense than for Mock Doy to kill Corbett for that act? He could take the blame and both would be dead.

"I like it," he said aloud again. "It will work."

With his plan thought out, he again let his mind focus on White Lotus. He liked that name. It suited the girl better than Alley Cat. When she accepted her position as his personal *ah mah*, he would see that she was adorned in immaculate white silk. Once she learned her responsibilities he would know her soft, yielding body. The idea alone was enough to drive him crazy. As soon as Corbett was out of the way, the girl would be his.

A slat opened along the upper portion of the door and an eye appeared at the peephole.

"We no open," a Chinese voice said from the other side. "Go 'way."

"Open up, me friend," Rusty ordered, "or I'll smash that door into firewood!"

"No open!" the man cried. "No open!"

Rusty did not ask what Reese wanted to do. He turned a shoulder toward the door and rammed into it with the force of a runaway freight train. The door ripped the inner lock loose from the frame and flew back to smack into the man on the other side, knocking him off his feet.

A woman screamed, and there was a mad shuffling of feet. Reese plunged into the room, but it was empty. He rushed into a narrow hallway, but discovered only more doors. Yanking open one after another revealed nothing but empty compartments.

"What the heck?" he asked aloud. "Where'd they go?"

Rusty marched past him and studied the inner wall. With no warning, he kicked a hole in the wall. That act prompted a girl's muffled scream. He tore several boards loose to show a neat little hiding place between the wall partitions.

The girl, however, was not Alley Cat. She cringed back from them and chattered something in Chinese.

"It's not her," Reese told Rusty.

"Let's have a look in the next room," the big man suggested. "If she's here, we'll round her up."

Reese found the trapdoor in the next room. It was hidden under a rug. When he pulled it open, he discovered an empty chamber. Rusty had the same luck in the next room. Before they could investigate the last door, an elderly Chinese woman confronted them. Four tough-looking men were at her sides.

"You go away!" she ordered. "Go away, man. I pay vely good to protection!"

There was no time to answer or challenge her command. The four Chinese rushed upon them, wielding long-bladed knives and short clubs.

Reese ducked away from one in front as the man took a vicious swing at him with a club. Dodging to the side, Reese caught hold of his arm. He jerked the man forward and wrestled him to the floor. Rusty did not back up, but charged headlong into the others.

Rolling over with his man, Reese gave his assailant's wrist a violent twist and shook the club out of his hand. A chopping hand flashed toward the base of Reese's neck, but he flinched enough to take the brunt of the blow on his shoulder. He drove his own fist into the face of his assailant, squashing his nose flat.

The man grunted in pain and bucked Reese off him. As he tried to turn onto his stomach, Reese grabbed the club. Before the man could rise, Reese clouted him hard on the side of the head.

The man had been almost to his knees, but the blow stunned him. Even as he sought to crawl away, Reese hammered him on top of the skull a second time and knocked him flat onto the floor. He was out of the fight, so Reese looked to Rusty, expecting he would need help with the other three.

But Rusty had caught hold of one of the attackers by his shirtfront. With a mighty heave, he hauled him off his feet and hurled him into the other two. It made their weapons useless. As Reese climbed over the one he had downed, Rusty pounced into the middle of the other three. He was a wild man, smashing faces as if he were a brawling cyclone.

Reese had to get out of his way, as Rusty latched on to one of the men's pigtails and yanked him off his feet. The man's head crashed into the wall, and he dropped limply to the floor.

Recalling Rusty's boast about being able to whip ten men, Reese realized that there had been little exaggeration in that claim.

Once the last henchman was piled with the others, the woman disappeared into the last room down the hallway, but Rusty and Reese followed too quickly for her to make her escape out the window. She twisted in Rusty's grasp and screamed for help, but no one came to her aid.

"Where is the girl known as Alley Cat?" Reese demanded. "What have you done with her?"

The madam shook her head. "Get out! Not know!"

Rusty pushed the woman over for Reese to restrain and searched the room from corner to corner. He located another trapdoor, concealed by a rug. He had to move the bed to get to it, and tossed it aside like a piece of paper. When he lifted up the false section of floor, Reese spotted someone bound and gagged. Hair hid her face, but he recognized the green robe over silk pajamas.

"She the one?" Rusty asked.

Recognizing the small, frightened face, Reese felt instant relief. "That's her."

The big man straddled the hole and took hold of the girl. As he lifted her up, the madam bolted from the room. Reese let her go, moving over at once to untie Cat.

With only her hands free, she wrapped her arms around him and clung to him. It made it hard to even get the knot out of the cloth that was tied around her mouth. He fumbled with it for a moment, then it came free.

Rusty laughed at the sight. "I'll be a-thinking that you've gone and got yourself a woman, sonny. She has a set notion for you like a bear after a honeycomb."

"I—I thought they'd—that they'd killed you!" she said, trembling within his arms.

He stood awkwardly, uncertain of what to do or say. He patted Alley Cat on the back.

Rusty was openly amused. "Is it burping a baby you are, sonny?" He laughed. "By the saints! Give the lassy a decent hug. Then maybe she'll let us get out of here before that turtle woman brings an entire tong down on our necks."

The girl saved Reese further embarrassment, pushing back a full step from him. "I'm sorry," she murmured.

Reese cleared his throat to get his voice to work, while taking hold of her hand. "Let's get moving. We don't want another fight on our hands."

Rusty grunted at his remark. "You'll be a-speaking for yourself, sonny. I'm just gettin' loosened up meself."

"Take the lead, Rusty."

"Aye, I'll lead the way," he said. "But it's wondering I am that you have so many more enemies than friends."

The three of them stepped over the four groggy Chinese, who were still trying to get their senses back. Then they hurried out the door and down a narrow alley. Within minutes, they were in the white part of town and out of danger.

"What now?" Rusty asked as they paused to catch their wind.

"Now we get her some decent clothes," Reese replied.

"Purty as a pixie, if you was to ask me," Rusty replied.

"Well," Reese said defensively, "she isn't a joy girl, so she shouldn't have to dress like one."

The big man raised his bushy eyebrows. "Whatever you say, lad."

Alley Cat looked at Reese, moved by his gallantry.

Reese asked Rusty, "Where can we stay in relative safety?"

"Betty Mae's Boardinghouse. She fixes a fine breakfast and supper that goes with the room. I've stayed there when the weather was too bad to camp out, or on the rare occasion when I wanted to eat someone's cooking besides me own."

"I'm running low on funds," Reese admitted. "I ought to wire my boss for some more expense money. All I have is a couple of gold coins from the poke I had stuck in my shirt. After buying back my own horse and with what I need for the lady, I'm going to be about broke."

"Lucky that lynch mob missed the pouch," Rusty said.

"They took my pocket money and would have probably gotten my badge too, if not for the fact that I keep it pinned to the inside of my boot."

Rusty stuck a meaty paw into his own pocket. "I still have a little left from those four horses you helped me acquire. Besides that, I took me five-hundred commission for delivering that money to the bank for Grayson. We've no worry about money yet."

"I can't let you . . ."

The big man held up his hand to prevent argument. "My treat," he said firmly. "It's been one good time you've been a-showing me, since I met up with you, sonny." He guffawed good-naturedly. "How many other mates would cut me in on the kind of excitement I've had with you?"

"You could have gotten killed helping me up at Grayson's place and again back there in that brothel."

He showed a mountain-man grin. " 'Tis exactly what I'm a-saying, sonny. You add more spice to a man's life than a wagon full of cinnamon."

"Lead the way to that boardinghouse. I have an awful headache and I'm sure Cathy could use some rest."

"You called me Cathy," the girl said softly as they began to follow Rusty.

"Sounds better than Cat, don't you think?" He checked the expression on her upturned face to be sure he hadn't offended her.

"It is very nice, very . . . American." She smiled.

As they made their way toward the boardinghouse, several women on the street were quick to utter rude remarks or point at her. It took restraint for Reese not to stop and give them a tongue-lashing that would strip the hide from their pious bones. After enduring the insults in silence, Cat finally broke down.

"Mr. Corbett," Cat's voice was as soft as that of a small child, "why did you bother to come after me?"

He tried to think of a suitable answer to her question. Getting the girl back had been paramount on his mind, but he could not explain the exact reason. He needed an interpreter, but there were others Kim Lee probably could suggest. He had jeopardized his entire mission by rescuing the girl a second time.

She continued to belabor the subject. "Half of the Chinese population in the state will know that you have taken me from the tong who claim me as their property. You will be in constant danger."

"You talk too much," he growled.

She refused to let the matter drop. "But you risked your life to come into the Chinese district. Why should you do that?"

He shot her a hard glance. Surprisingly, she did not shrink from his gaze. Rather, she looked up at him, her somber, cloudy-blue eyes visible through the black locks of her hair.

"You should trim your hair out of your eyes," he said, changing the subject completely. "Stop hiding your face."

She knit her eyebrows. "Do what?"

"And we're going to stop in the next store, too," he continued. "You are going to get yourself some fashionable clothes, shoes, and whatever else a proper young lady should have. It's high time you quit being ashamed of having mixed blood."

"But—"

"No buts!"

CHAPTER 9

QUAN PACED THE floor and cursed the gods. Tin Hau, the queen of heaven, had not smiled on him since Reese Corbett had come onto the scene. Next, Kwan Kung, the god of war, had not put strength in his own men's swords. They had been badly beaten at the joy house.

Ti Kong's face was swollen and discolored. He stood solemnly, not speaking a word since he had informed Quan of the disastrous confrontation with the two Americans.

"Who is this huge wild man, the one called Rusty?"

"He used to be a freight driver, but has been working independently for the past few months. I believe his loyalty to Corbett is due to the man saving him from ambush."

"How are the others?"

"Corbett used a club on Ah Gow, but he will recover."

"When is Mock Doy due back?"

"Maybe tomorrow. Do you wish me to prepare an ambush?"

"No, I have something else in mind for him."

"But Mock has been working behind your back. He—"

Quan held up a fleshy palm. "I think Mock is the man to rid us of Corbett's interference. You get word to him to follow Corbett. If he gets the chance, he is to try and kill him. If not, he is to warn Wyngate of both the lawman and that big bear friend of his."

"I told one of his men up at the tollhouse that a lawman was snooping about. He should be wary of any strangers."

"Good."

"What can we do about the girl?"

Quan let out a sigh of resignation. "We can do nothing at the moment. Once Corbett is out of the way, she will be without aid or friendship. We will take her back at that time."

"We can no longer follow the two men while they are in the white part of town," Ti told him. "A Chinese would be conspicuous in that part of the city."

"I have some connections," Quan replied. "I will keep track of our friends until they leave town again. When he returns, have Mock Doy stand ready to follow at once."

"You think Corbett will find out anything?"

"We have been careful, Ti, but there are many eyes and ears along our route. Someone has probably seen the covered wagons that roll at night and wondered about them. Another alert person might have heard some voices, or been curious about the shipments of rice and dried fish to an unknown destination." Quan folded his arms in contemplation. "Our best defense is to be rid of Mr. Corbett and his large friend."

"It will be as you wish," Ti said. "I will find Mock Doy and instruct him. As for Mock meeting his own destiny"— Ti showed a mirthless grin—"I will await your order to settle with him."

Quan nodded. "Yes, Mock will need to be around, should there be any suspicions cast against the Chinese population. He will be here to accept the blame."

"I'll be on my way, Quan. Ah Gow and the others are recovering at the casino, should you need someone."

"Swift feet and safe journey," Quan told him.

Once Ti was out of the room, Quan considered his situation. Reese Corbett had caused him a great deal of trouble. His snatching Alley Cat right out of the joy house was something for which he wanted to make the man pay. For years, he had watched Alley Cat scurry about like a pack-rat. He had watched her grow and mature into a nubile young woman. He had been patient, and now she was a rare jewel, a rough diamond that needed only polish to sparkle like the brightest of stars.

He bit down hard, anger flooding his veins with hate and desire for vengeance. Reese Corbett was all that stood in his way. The deputy marshal had taken the girl from him twice, and he was meddling about in Quan's lucrative slave trade. The man was more trouble to him than a horde of fleas to a dog.

"Not for much longer," he said aloud. "Your time on this earth has almost expired, Mr. Corbett. And your end cannot come too soon to suit me!"

Reese left Cat at her room, along with her purchases and a tub of hot water. Rusty was waiting patiently for him. Reese decided it was time to have a talk with the big man. Rusty had saved him from a deadly beating, forked over money to buy him a horse at Grayson's place, then shelled out more money at the boardinghouse. The man had more than paid him back, both in physical help and financial aid.

"What now?" Rusty said, ready to follow Reese once more.

"Let's grab a cup of mud."

"Sounds good."

When they had been served and were alone, Reese fixed a steady gaze on Rusty. Reese tested the coffee, but it was too hot to even sip. He sorted his words, uncertain of how to proceed.

"You have stuck your neck out to help me twice. You no longer owe me for helping you out of that ambush."

"Be you saying 'tis time to put the team in a dual-harness, sonny?"

"Not exactly, but it is time for me to get on with my job. I've got to look into the disappearance of a number of Chinese workers. We suspect that someone is dealing in slaves, and I have to get to the bottom of it."

"Sounds like a noble undertaking."

"It's my job."

"And you be in this investigation alone?"

"So far. I haven't learned anything yet, so there's no need to request help until I have leads or evidence of some kind."

"Do you not think that I could be of some help? I know a good many people. Mayhaps you could let me give you a hand."

"Why would you want to?" Reese asked. "It isn't your job, and it might mean risking you neck."

"Methinks that I ain't done nothing for nobody but meself for a long time, sonny. That makes a man's life near worthless, always looking out only for himself.

"Well, I got to thinking about that little Alley Cat. She ain't never had a chance in life. I remember seeing her once, a few years back. I was a-riding through the Chinese district and happened to see a bunch of kids throwing rocks at her, chasing her down the street. I'm a-thinking that white kids and Chinese kids alike have teased and tormented her since she was a wee lassie. I've had my share of troubles, but I was always big enough to stand up for meself. Not the lassie."

"Tough being an outcast in society," Reese spoke up. "And now that she is older, Quan wants to make a slave out of her."

"That's what I been a-saying, sonny. You and me can make a difference. You and that Kim Lee are trying to do something good for these Chinese. That is worthwhile, something to be proud of." He gave his head a shake. "I figure to be about as tough as forged steel, but I've never done me nothing to make me folks proud. I'm offering to side with you in this here shindig."

"The thing is, if you've a mind to continue helping me, you ought to have a badge. This is a matter for the law."

"A marshal be unable to do the things I can, sonny.

Your hands are tied by your oath to uphold the law. I can do whatever else is needed to get the job done." He flashed his usual grin. "We can make an unbeatable team, we can."

"If you are determined to see this through, I could use your help," Reese told him. "But I can't stand by and watch while you do anything illegal. A man who upholds the law has to abide by all laws, not just the one he is trying to enforce."

Rusty grinned. "Aye, I know what you're telling me. Where do we start?"

Reese sent Rusty toward the docks to ask questions and do some snooping around. Then Reese went to the clerk and recorder's office.

He spent an hour talking to the head clerk and looking through filed claims, deeds, and a host of records. Hoy Quan's name appeared on one of the titles and also one deed. There was nothing in the records to indicate that he was involved in running any kind of operation that was crooked or unusual.

Reese returned to the street. He visited a couple of the local banks, one of the major importers, and several freighting companies. He met up with Rusty late that day and listened to what the man had learned.

"In the past," Rusty told him, "the Chinese coming in were represented by a sponsor who put up fifty bucks for the trip. The worker had to repay two hundred. Most of them agreed to work under a bond or some such thing, until they paid off the debt. After that, they were free to work for themselves."

"And lately?"

"Someone on this end be putting up the fee for a whole bunch of workers, without asking for a bond."

"You find out which import companies were still bringing in workers?"

"Our Chinese gent, Quan, is out front like the lead steer on a trail drive, making all the arrangements for the gathering of labor gangs. 'Tis nothing but a hunch and an itch I can't scratch about this, but I be a-thinking Quan is only stirring up the dust to hide the real bull of the herd. That would be the fellow with the money. Man who owns the merchant ship is Cyrus Brown. He be a local judge."

"A judge," Reese considered. "That's interesting, Rusty. I happened to see the name Cyrus Brown at the land office. He is part owner of a mining company. He and some fellow named Wyngate have filed claims at a place called Gold Spur, up near that rough country back in Snake Canyon."

"Fellow at the dock told me that the judge done got himself a regular mansion on the north side of town. Be you thinking he is not quite on the level?"

"Let's say that it would appear that the man throws a wide loop. Who would know where those laborers were taken, once they were off the ship?"

"I know a good many freighters about town," Rusty suggested. "If you're of a mind, I'll make the rounds and see if any of them know who might be hauling the coolies and where they be a-taking them."

"That would be a real help. We need a starting point, but don't let on as to why you're looking for that information. If they get wise to us and cover their tracks, it'll be twice as hard to find out anything."

"Aye, I'll tread as softly as a field mouse in a snake pit, sonny. You need have no worry about me."

"All right. I'll meet you back at the boardinghouse later."

The big man lumbered off and Reese silently thanked Lady Luck that he had run into Rusty McCune. Having been a freighter, he would know where to look and who to talk to. His footwork was saving Reese a great deal of time and effort.

Reese decided not to question the judge, just in case he was involved in the illegal trafficking of coolies. It stood to reason that this missing-persons case might be a part of something very big. A few missing Chinese was one thing, but this had the earmarks of a much larger-scale operation. There was someone involved in shipping the Chinese in from overseas, several more mixed up with the transporting of them to an unknown destination, and another man on the receiving end of the deal. If Lee was correct in assuming that there might be several hundred Chinese involved, Reese could be up against a small army, run by someone with money and power.

Cyrus Brown had the power. As a judge, he could produce the needed documents and pull a few key strings concerning dock police and local officials. Quan could make the contacts to get the coolie laborers from Hong Kong to San Francisco. Quan was also head of a huge network of tongs, able to silence or soothe any objections that might arise from the Chinese community. That would explain why it was a man like Lee who was receiving letters and voicing a complaint. He was the only one with the money and clout to stand against Quan.

Reese was still in the dark as to where the Chinese were going and why they were being taken in the first place. As he started to walk back to the boardinghouse, he again wondered what Cat had to do with anything. Was she in a position to know what had happened to those missing men? If so, there was a chance someone would try to silence her once and for all.

Reese was also curious about the men who had tailed him. *How did they know I would be coming? Why take the girl? And why not kill me, instead of leaving me behind?*

His mind turned over angles and possibilities. When he tried to work the dilemma into something that made sense, nothing fit. It was similiar to a puzzle all of one color, with all the pieces cut the same size. There was no starting point.

He entered the boardinghouse and went up to his room.

When he opened the door, he was dumbfounded to find Cat waiting for him. He stood in awe, his mouth agape.

She had been sitting on the edge of his bed, her hands patiently folded in her lap, and she rose uncertainly to face him. Her hair had been brushed to a healthy, radiant black sheen, the locks no longer concealing her face, but straight and evenly cropped along her forehead. She wore a yellow chiffon dress, held snug at the waist by a matching yellow sash.

He gulped down his wonder and blinked. It took no little effort to recover his voice. Mesmerized, he woodenly stepped into the room and eased the door closed.

"Great day in the morning, Cathy!" he exclaimed breathlessly. "You look beautiful."

Cat ducked her head demurely, a rush of color flooding her cheeks at his praise.

He sought to regain a bit of dignity. "I mean . . . that dress sure enough suits you."

She turned around slowly, allowing him to inspect her outfit. "It is a very pretty dress."

"I'm glad Rusty picked it out."

"Odd for a man like him to choose something so fancy, so very feminine. I was shocked that he would even enter that part of the store."

"He's a unique fellow, all right."

"I shouldn't think there would be anyplace to wear this, other than a dance or a party," she said. "I would hate to ever get it dirty."

"That's why we bought the other dress," he replied, thinking of the plain gray cotton dress she had picked out by herself.

Cat moved silently over to stand within his reach. When she looked up at him, her eyes were a deeper blue than before. It was strange, but the color of her irises appeared to change with her mood.

"You paid a lot of money for me," she said directly.

"Then you came all the way back here and risked your life to take me from the Garden of Love. Why did you do that?"

"I told you right off," he said.

"That you needed an interpreter?"

"Yeah, that's it exactly."

A coolness crept into her eyes. "And you rescued me for only that reason?"

"Well . . ." He could not think straight. "Yeah, that's right. I needed someone who could talk the lingo, someone who wouldn't be suspected."

There was an immediate change in her manner, something he could not comprehend. "Will I need this dress?"

"Maybe so, but I think the other one will be . . ."

"Then I will change," she said shortly.

"You don't have to do that," he protested at once. "We can go . . ."

But she was no longer looking at him or listening to him. She pushed past him and went out the door. When it closed behind her, it was with enough force that the window in the room rattled.

"Reese, old buddy," he said aloud, his momentary elation crushed by his own awkward handling of the situation. "All the time you was growing up, you never did have a way with women. It's plain to see that time and maturity ain't changed that one bit."

CHAPTER 10

AFTER THE EVENING meal, Reese held a meeting in his room. Rusty plopped down on his bed, sitting next to Cat. She wore the gray dress, was very subdued, and refused to make eye contact with Reese. Worse, she was taciturn, as if absorbed in only her own thoughts.

Reese leaned back against the wall and got down to business. "What did you learn from the freighters, Rusty? Were you able to pick up any helpful information?"

"Everything be pretty hush-hush," he replied. "The only thing I learned is that there is a big shipment of rice and dried fish leaving town every week. It be sent by wagon to Grayson's Tollhouse, then it be transferred to pack mules."

"Pack mules?"

He nodded. "No one was to be a-knowing where it goes from there, but one of me old mates thinks it ends up at Gold Spur."

"Are they working any mines up that way yet?"

"Nothing as far as anyone knows. 'Twas like me story about getting back to that new place, sonny. It runs around the edge of a towering mountain. 'Twould take months to carve a road, if that even be possible. Those jagged peaks are solid rock and a thousand feet higher than the winding path they use now."

"Then a mining operation would have to be all by hand, and the ore would have to come out on pack mules."

"Be one slow process," Rusty replied. "Exceptional ore might bring upwards of a hundred dollars a ton. Each pack mule could only pack about three hundred pounds. It don't take too much ciphering to see that there would be a need for a great number of mules to do the job that way."

"Be tough to make any money, even if the ore was top grade."

"Aye, and I told you afore about the characters that sometimes come down to Grayson's place. Whoever is running the operation has the toughest crew of men ever put together."

"Any idea how many men are up there altogether?"

Rusty toyed with the end of his bushy beard, knitting his dark brows in thought. "I'd be not knowing for certain, sonny. There is supposed to be several mines back in the hills near Grayson's place, but if they are being worked or not is a bit of a question. As for the place we be talking about, Gold Spur, me guess would be that there are maybe a dozen of those hardcase characters."

"That wouldn't be enough to do much mining."

"No," Rusty agreed. "And them fellows pack a lot of iron. There be not any miners among them."

"Not miners?"

"Those lads could break rocks with their fists, but I'll be a-thinking they are mostly guards or walking bosses for labor gangs."

"But you just said that no one knows of any large-scale digging back along the Snake Canyon?"

"Aye. If there was serious mining going on, they would need rail and ore carts, timber for shoring up, material for running air venting, and a host of wheels, cables, ropes, and the like. I took me a tour into the Comstock mine one time. That dig runs well over a thousand feet deep in places. I've seen for meself how much special equipment is needed."

"And nothing like that is being hauled to Gold Spur?"

"Only a goodly supply of black powder."

"Might that be for that road that is being built? Any information on it?"

"Only rumors. But I'll not be seeing how anyone can build a road on the sheer side of a cliff. The trail is little more than a ledge, maybe as narrow as four feet in a lot of places. One rock slide and there won't be any way back into those hills atall. Makes it tough to imagine how they are using that powder."

Reese considered this. "I was with the railroad for a short time. I remember them tunneling through a mountain that was like solid granite. Twenty-four hours a day they attacked that stone wall with picks and tons of explosives, and it was seldom they made more than a foot-a-day progress. The use of manpower was enormous."

A glimmer shone in Rusty's eyes. "And most of that work was done by Chinese workers."

"If a man was to put a road through that first big mountain, how tough would it be to make a freight wagon run back into Snake Canyon?"

"The way would be clear," Rusty replied. "That great wall of solid rock is the only real problem."

"How about you, Cathy?" he asked the girl. "Did anyone mention anything about the place you were supposed to go?"

"Only that we were going to a new joy house," she said quietly.

"No names of people or places?"

"No."

"What's the plan, sonny?" Rusty showed a renewed enthusiasm.

"We are going to need a cover of some kind, to get back into Gold Spur without arousing suspicion. Most of those guys at Grayson's hardly looked at me twice. They had eyes only for the girls. There was no moon for the ones who caught me at the road to see me by. I'll have to hope that no one recognizes me. And I can't ride in there with a badge showing, for that would be asking for trouble."

" 'Tis no argument you'll get from me there," he agreed. "What's the answer?"

Reese did some quick thinking. "I think I can get us to Snake Canyon without being suspect."

"What about the wee princess here?" Rusty wanted to know. "With her being at that there auction, them sots at Grayson's place probably took a pretty good look at her."

"Maybe none of the men were down from the Snake that night."

Rusty shook his head. "That isn't something you can take for granted."

Reese stared at the girl for a moment. "With her hair pulled back and wearing that dress, I doubt anyone would recognize her. After all, she was made up like a Chinese joy girl, with white powder all over her face and red rouge on her cheeks and lips."

"That's a point taken right well."

"Besides," Reese allowed himself a smile, "no one will dare give her a second look, once they know who she is."

The girl, finally too curious not to take notice, peeked up at Reese. Rusty also leaned forward in anticipation.

"So who is she going to be?"

"She is going to be a missionary's wife."

Lowell Wyngate enjoyed his power. He watched the two Chinese men endure twenty lashes each, satisfied that it was a good lesson for all of the others. They would think twice about trying to escape again.

Dorty Keats, his foreman, gave the signal to stop the beating. He then looked to Wyngate for instructions.

"Leave them bound to the poles until dark. Make sure that everyone on the shift change walks past them. I want those coolies to know that I won't tolerate any further escape attempts."

Keats gave the order, then joined Wyngate. He was lean and tough as braided rawhide, with no conscience, no nerves, no compassion. Money was the only way of buying his loyalty. Five hundred dollars a month was his price, and he was worth every penny.

"I spoke to that chink, Ti Kong, down at Grayson's the other night," he told Wyngate. "He said that there was a U.S. marshal investigating some missing highbinders. What do you think?"

"We'll double the guard at the trail entrance."

"That will run us short at the tunnel."

"Can't be helped. We don't want someone snooping around. Too much is at stake."

Keats tipped his hat to shade his eyes from the afternoon sun. "I see your two boys are back from their bank raid."

"You mean Razor and the Kid?"

"I wouldn't trust either of them to dot the i's in idiot," Keats said tightly. "One of the boys heard that they took six thousand dollars over at the Silver Thorn bank. They brought in less than four."

"They take the risks, so they have to be paid more money."

"Thirty percent?"

Wyngate did not like Keats second-guessing him, but the man was important to the success of the job.

"Can't expect to hire crooks and then have them be on the level with you, Keats. That bank job will pay you and the men for another two months."

"They shot up the town pretty bad, boss."

"I don't tell them how to rob banks," Wyngate replied tightly. "We needed more money for operating expenses. That seventy to a hundred barrels of black powder a day doesn't come cheap."

"I know that, boss," Keats admitted. "But I don't like having a couple of rabid dogs around. Razor Back is about as crazy as a horse on loco weed. He enjoys killing."

"We only need to get through the Old Maid."

"Rate we're going, the country will dry up and blow away before we ever get through that mountain of rock."

"We need more nitroglycerin."

"It's against the law to bring it into California, Lowell. That makes it tougher to keep in supply."

"You'll have to tell the chemist that we need more production from him."

"We've got glycerin enough, but he run out of both nitric and sulphuric acids. He expects more tomorrow or the next day. Then he'll whip off a new batch."

Wyngate removed a thick cigar from his pocket and stuck it between his lips. He never had acquired the taste of smoke, but he did enjoy chewing on the end of an imported cigar. It helped him to relax, to ponder his options and think over important matters.

"Six months," he sighed. "Another measly foot yesterday. Twelve inches to show for twenty-four hours' work. That's the difference of using regular powder, Keats."

"Ain't no doubt that we need more nitro, Lowell. I checked with the shift bosses. There was no slacking off. The crews worked solid the entire time. The Old Maid is sure enough made out of the hardest rock I ever seen."

"Millions in gold are in these mountains, Keats. We only need that miserable road and we'll be on our way."

"If we ever get through, it'll be a wonder. I don't think we're quite halfway yet."

"We need more men," Wyngate said. "There were delays yesterday, when we didn't have the manpower to move the rubble from that big morning blast. We lost several hours during the cleanup process."

"Seventy men to a shift, Lowell. Can't hardly get more than that into the tunnel at one time."

"But the cost! We're running out of places to get money!"

"How about Quan?"

"He has sold most of his holdings already."

"And Cyrus?"

"His shipping line is mortgaged to the bank. There will be a payment due in several weeks. He expects us to come up with enough ore to pay that bill."

"What ore? We ain't taken anything but samples. They look good, but it sure won't pay any big mortgage payment."

"We'll find a way."

"You going to send out Razor and the Kid again?"

"Too many lawmen looking for them right now. They need to lay low for a spell."

"I couldn't help but notice that they about took over the two girls you brought up for company."

Wyngate set his teeth, thinking of that. "Yeah, the idea was for the two girls to entertain all of the men. I'm beginning to think it wasn't such a good idea. Been three or four fights already."

"That won't be the half of it, if Razor and the Kid stick around for any length of time. Someone will end up getting killed. That Razor is a crazy fool and the albino follows his lead like his pet dog."

"Crazy or not, we still need the money they provide. Wish that third girl hadn't escaped. At least then we would have one extra girl to entertain the other men."

"Give the word, and I'll lay down some rules to Razor and the Kid." Keats tapped his gun butt. "If it came right down to it, I could probably take them both in a gunfight."

Wyngate did not like that idea. "The time might come for that, Keats, but not yet. Like I said, we still need those two, especially after what you told me about Quint and the three Vougal brothers being killed in that ambush the other day. I was counting on the money that was being shipped from Grayson's place."

"Hard to say what went wrong, boss. That Ti Kong told me that he witnessed the four of them being killed by that same marshal who is doing the snooping around. Him and the big guy gunned them all down."

"I'll ask around next time I'm at the tollhouse and check that story. Hard to believe that all four were killed in the fight."

"What about the U.S. marshal? If he starts sniffing around up here, it won't take long to find out that we have been tapping resources from a dozen directions to pay for our tunnel."

"Like I said, double the guard at the trail and we'll keep an eye on anyone who comes sniffing around."

Keats left to do as he was told. Wyngate watched him, but his mind was not on his foreman. He was concerned that Razor Back and the Albino Kid had skimmed so much of the money. The gold-mine business was looking worse all the time. When viewed logically, the pie he had baked was going to be cut into so many slices there would be little for any of them. Cyrus, Quan, the two bank robbers, and himself. That was splitting it five ways to start with.

He made a decision concerning Razor and the Kid. They did not need to be cut in on any deal. When they had served their purpose, they would pay him one last dividend—the price on their heads.

Striding toward the main hut, he spotted the two Chinese girls. They were washing their clothes, chattering back and forth in their native tongue. He slowed his pace, enjoying the sight.

He had visited a joy house once before, but he was not satisfied to pay for an hour or a night with a girl. He wanted something more from a woman. He would soon be rich and powerful. A man like that did not want a second-hand woman, one who had known many men. She would have to be pure as the newest snow on the high peaks. He would share her with no one, and she would serve only his needs. Whether she became his wife or not would depend on how the relationship progressed. Either his wife or his mistress, he would have her only for himself.

Once the mine was shelling out millions of dollars' worth of ore, he would have everything he had ever wanted. At the thought, he turned and glared at the monster mountain of rock, the Old Maid. She was one tough customer: stern, toweringly resolute, unyielding. If only they could manage to finish the road. That was all that was holding them back. She was all that stood between him and his dreams of wealth and grandeur.

CHAPTER 11

REESE CHECKED HIS timepiece and walked toward the general store. They needed to get moving. It was an overnight trip to Grayson's Tollhouse, then another full day into Snake Canyon. Rusty had most of the supplies loaded and was ready to go. Cat had only needed to pick up a few items. She should have been back by now.

Even as he entered the front of the store, he could see the problem. A middle-aged lady, in fashionable dress and a wide-brimmed, flowered hat, was at the counter. She was giving the owner what-for, while Cat appeared cowed by the woman, her head ducked, eyes lowered.

". . . let this riffraff ruin the reputation of your store," the woman was saying haughtily. "I can tell you, James, I'm of a mind to take my business over to Dougherty's Mercantile. He has a sign on the door that forbids Indians or Chinese from entering."

Reese moved past the counter and picked up a can of peaches. He then stepped up behind Cat. "I'm sorry, Mrs. Brown," the storekeeper apologized.

"Excuse me, madam," Reese said to the woman. "I wonder if you would mind putting a leash on your high-falutin venom. You're holding up the line."

She glared hotly at Reese. "You have some nerve, young man!" she snapped. "Perhaps you are ignorant of the fact that my husband is Judge Brown!"

"I'll extend him my sympathy, next time I see him, ma'am," he replied seriously.

She sucked in her breath, shocked and appalled at his affront. Rather than counter his rude remark, she stormed out of the front door and marched briskly off down the walk.

Once she was out of sight, Reese put a questioning look to the man behind the counter.

"You open for business, or is our money no good here?"

The man made an effort to close his mouth. His head bobbed up and down quickly. "Certainly, sir. Whatever you like. I believe the young lady here was next."

Cat paid for her purchases, out of the money Rusty had provided. Once Reese had also paid for his tin of peaches, they left the store together.

"Don't ever let some pious, uppity woman with no manners belittle you," he said, as they walked toward Rusty and the horses.

"But"—she shook her head in confusion—"that was Mrs. Brown! She is a proper lady. She is—"

"She's a haughty, pretentious old witch!" he declared vehemently. "You listen to me, Cathy. You are every bit as good as anyone else!"

Reese wondered why he felt such intense anger over the incident. Cat had grown used to such treatment by the white population. She had taken the woman's ridicule and belittling in subdued silence. But he felt a fury within his chest that would not be quelled. He did not understand why people felt they had the right to talk down to someone like Cat, as if she were some form of lower life.

Rusty had the horses saddled and waiting. He came forward to take a few items Cat had bought at the store. After sticking them into a supply sack, he frowned at Reese.

"Are you going to nibble on that airtight of fruit along the way?"

Reese looked dumbly at the tin of peaches in his hand. He tossed it to Rusty.

"Forgot I even had it."

The big man added the can to the supplies and secured

the sack in place on the pack animal. Reese took a moment to give Cat a leg up onto her horse. He could not help but notice that she was awkward and outwardly apprehensive, even as she squirmed into position in the saddle.

"I have never ridden a horse solo before," she said meekly.

"We'll be a-taking it slow and easy, lassie," Rusty replied. "It be a long ride ahead. 'Tis a master of the fair steed you'll be long before we get to Gold Spur."

Reese adjusted her stirrups for length and double-checked the saddle cinch. Cat tied a poke bonnet into place, while he mounted up on Dancer.

"It's been on me mind to mention your horse, sonny," Rusty remarked, looking at Dancer. "I've not been a-seeing many of them palomino ponies around. I'd always heard that they didn't have any staying power."

"Depends on how you treat them. I've run down a number of hard-riding men on his back."

"Well, I'll be watching to see that you keep up." He grinned. "Let's put some tracks between us and this here town. Got a long haul ahead of us."

Cat was at the edge of the creek. She had only intended to wash, but seeking relief for her saddle-sore limbs, she began to apply the cold water to the inside of her legs. At someone's approach, she quickly pulled the hem of her dress down to her ankles.

" 'Tis a wee rough getting used to riding." Rusty's voice was friendly and sympathetic.

She glanced over her shoulder at him and forced a weary smile. "Yes," she admitted. "The stirrups rubbed me raw."

" 'Tis some liniment I brung you," he said, holding out a bottle of clear liquid. "Fact is, Corbett had it in his tack."

She accepted the bottle and gave him a curious look. "So why didn't he offer it to me?"

Rusty hunkered down on his haunches and ran his fingers through the curls at the end of his beard. When he spoke, he kept his voice low enough that his words would not travel beyond her own ears.

"I'm for thinking sonny is not real experienced with the fair sex, Cat." He paused to turn his head and spit a stream of tobacco juice into the dirt. Then he shook his head. "Rotten habit, chewing and spitting. Hope you don't mind putting up with it."

"There are worse habits," she said.

"Like I was saying, we has got to watch over that boy, Cat. He's not a-knowing yet what is best for him."

"And what is best for him?"

He winked at her. "We both know the answer to that question, but it ain't stuck in his own head yet."

She felt a wave of warm blood rush to heat her face. "I . . . I don't think I . . ."

"Like giving you this here bottle of liniment." Rusty appeared to ignore her own reaction. "He is afraid of being alone with you. 'Tis my thinking that the boy has been snakebit"—he grinned, shifting the chaw of tobacco from one cheek to the other—"if you don't mind me referring to you as a snake."

She offered him a slight smile. "Thank you . . . for the liniment."

Rusty raised a hand to bid farewell and lumbered back toward the campfire. Cat watched him go, experiencing an inner warmth. He was a big, burly bear of a man, but nothing in his makeup was any larger than his heart.

Turning to the chore at hand, she applied the liniment to the red, tender flesh along the inside of her legs. It burned on contact, but it soothed the fire after a few seconds. By the time she was ready to return to the firesite, she was able to walk almost normally.

She took a moment to study Reese as he laid out beds for the three of them. He had cut and trimmed boughs and had them neatly piled for bunks; he covered each with a ground blanket. From his handling of the beds, she knew that he had spent a great deal of time in the wilderness. He seemed so capable, so able to handle any given situation that might arise. Odd that Rusty should think that Reese was unsure of himself with a woman.

With the blankets in place, Reese discovered that Cat was standing right next to him. When he looked at her, she offered him a smile.

"Thank you for the liniment, Mr. Corbett," she said, holding the bottle out toward him.

"Better hang on to that," he told her, feeling suddenly self-conscious. "Tomorrow won't be any easier than the ride today."

"All right." She did not argue.

"I'm sorry we didn't have time to round up a decent woman's saddle. You're probably just about crippled from having to ride astraddle all day."

"I'll survive," she replied bravely.

"You're . . ." He had to clear his throat, for something had lodged at the base and constricted his words. "You're holding up well, for a first-time rider."

"I'm trying very hard not to be a burden to you."

"I doubt that you could ever be a burden to a man." He tried his hand at flattery. From the immediate crimson hue that came into her cheeks, he felt the line had been successful.

"You haven't told me much about this plan of yours," she said, changing the subject adroitly. "You said that I was to pretend to be your wife?"

"That's right. Rusty is the man we hired to guide us back to the Snake Canyon range," he explained. "I'm a missionary, carrying the Word of God to the heathen Chinese."

Her brows drew slightly together. "Heathens?"

"I didn't mean it like that," he admitted. "While you and Rusty were getting organized for the trip, I spent a couple of hours with Kim Lee. He told me a little about Chinese religion and customs. As they believe in a number of gods, we categorize them as heathen. I'm sure they probably believe we are equally ignorant by only worshiping one God."

"Are you really going to do missionary teaching?"

"I will read from the Good Book and you will translate. If anyone asks about your education, we'll tell them that you spent two years studying the language."

"There are a number of words in the Bible that I can't translate."

"Try and get close to the meanings. They won't know the difference. Besides that, the Bible is downright tough to decipher at times."

"And if they should hand me a writing of some kind?"

It was his turn to frown. "What about it?"

"I can't read a word of Chinese." She sighed and broke eye contact with him. "Matter of fact, I can't read English either. I never went to any of the mission schools."

"Don't worry about it," he said. "We'll try and keep things as simple as possible—for both of our sakes."

"How long will this take?"

"Hard to say," Reese told her truthfully. "If the men we find are all working for wages and know nothing about any of the missing coolies, we'll be moving on. There are other mining operations around that we can look into."

"Why do you suspect this one?"

"Hoy Quan is part owner of a mining claim on the Snake. Judge Cyrus Brown is also in partnership with the same man, a fellow called Wyngate. Cyrus owns the ship that is bringing in new labor gangs, and Quan is handling those arrangements in Hong Kong. That could tie them together in more than a simple human-import business."

"That isn't much to go on."

"According to Rusty, Wyngate has at least a dozen hired men on his payroll, hardcase types. Could be that they are used as guards or overseers to keep Chinese workers in line."

She appeared to concentrate on what he had told her. "When Mock Doy took me from the laundry, he also kidnapped the other two girls from a joy house. They did not know where they were being taken, but Mock Doy works for Quan."

"Exactly," Reese agreed. "Rusty told me that Wyngate was putting in a joy house for his men. With a big mining operation geared to start up, a casino would do a ripe business up there."

"They stole the girls for secrecy, but they might have been from Quan's own joy houses. No one would look for the stolen girls if they were not really missing."

"Sending his own girls would keep him from having trouble with another tong," Reese said, following the same line of thought.

"What about my being your wife?" Cat asked hesitantly.

The question threw him. He made an effort to maintain his outward poise, but his heart spooked like a frightened jackrabbit. He quieted the rapid pounding with no little effort.

"I'll present you as Mrs. Thompson. That will be our married name, Thompson."

"Why use a phony name?"

"There might be some hard cases who would recognize my real name. I've run down a few criminals in the state. It would only take one slip and we could get in big trouble real sudden."

Rather than question his motives further, the young woman parted her lips in a smile.

"Cathy Thompson," she said proudly. "I never had a real name before. Now I've got both a new first and last name."

Rusty cleared his throat gruffly, breaking into their conversation. "If it not be too much trouble, you two, I have got the meal cooked. If you'll be a-wanting your share, you best grab a plate." He chuckled, a throaty, bass chortle. "Come along, Mr. and Mrs. Thompson, before I throw it out."

As Reese picked up a plate, Rusty made a face and motioned him to move closer.

"What's up?"

" 'Tis an extra shadow among the trees," he said under his breath. "I've a mind to have a look-see."

"Want me to—"

"You and the lady give him something to watch. Keep our friend's attention until I get into the dark."

"All right," Reese agreed. "Be careful."

Rusty stood up and yanked the plate out of Reese's hand. "I'll not have you putting none of my cooking on that dirty tin," he complained loudly. "You'll not be blaming me for the bad taste, if it ain't from me own stewpot."

"What are you talking about?" Reese feigned insult. "I washed that there plate only last week!"

" 'Tis plain enough that you can't be a-doing nothing for yourself," Rusty countered. "I'll give it a good rinse in the creek and be right back."

Reese put his hands on his hips as the brute trudged off toward the stream. Cat came to stand alongside of him and regarded him with a curious look.

"What's the matter with Rusty?"

Reese shook his head. "Got me, Cathy. He's one of them fussy cooks, I guess." Then, leaning closer, he whispered, "We're being watched."

She stiffened noticeably, but was smart enough not to start looking around. Instead, she lowered her own plate. "What should we do?"

"Need to make us a little diversion," Reese said in a hushed voice.

"How?" she murmured softly.

"I'll attempt to kiss you," he decided. "You give me a little trouble and then slap me . . . just not too hard."

She appeared panic stricken. "But—but I—"

Reese took a quick look toward where Rusty had gone to wash the dish. Then he abruptly grabbed hold of Cat's arms. She dropped her plate and placed her hands against his chest.

"You've teased me long enough, Alley Cat," he said loudly. "Fight if you want, but I'm going to taste those inviting lips."

"No! Wait!" she objected with the appropriate amount of alarm in her voice. "Reese, I—"

He engulfed her with his arms, pulling her toward him. When his mouth found hers, he kissed her with reckless abandon.

Cat's hands pushed against his chest briefly, then—quite without warning—she yielded to him.

The shock of her returning his kiss stunned Reese, throwing him into a kind of elated trance. He became a prisoner to her, lost within the wondrous ardor of her embrace.

Then a gunshot resounded through the hills, shattering the stillness.

Reese and Cat jumped apart. He pulled his own gun and hurried off in the direction of the sound.

Rusty met him almost at once. He was reloading his pistol, as Reese slid to a stop in front of him.

"Got him," he said, holstering his gun easily. "Looks like one of those Chinese killers. He tried to use one of them big knives on me, a snickersnee, I believe they calls them."

Reese walked over to where the man and his short sword were lying together. He looked at him closely and straightened.

"Mock Doy!"

"He had a gun in his belt, but I surprised him. He whipped out that hacking sword instead of his pistol."

Rusty showed his contempt by spitting a stream of tobacco juice onto the fallen man. "Not very bright, him taking a swipe at me with one of those. What did he think, I'd use me skinning knife and try and beat him square?"

"He must have followed us from town."

"Think maybe Quan sent him?"

"Hard to say, Rusty. He's the one from the auction at Grayson's place. He might have wanted to either get even or steal Cathy back."

"Then his spying on us don't prove a thing."

"Afraid that's about it."

" 'Tis me thinking that we are not having the best of luck tracking down these lost pigtails of yours, sonny. When are you going to show me how you lawmen deduct from clues and that sort of thing?"

"I deduce that we're going to eat a cold meal—how's that?"

Rusty grunted sourly. "Big-hat reasoning there."

"What do you think we ought to do with his body?" Reese asked as Cat came softly padding into the woods to join them.

"Bury him right where he fell," Rusty said offhandedly. "Only one who will miss him is the man who hired him."

"It's Mock Doy?" Cat asked in surprise.

"He tried to separate Rusty's head from his body," Reese told her. "Mock won't be selling any more girls at any of the tollhouses."

"Was he after me?"

"We'll never know," Reese replied. "Rusty put his shot in a place that don't allow for questioning afterward."

" 'Twas me mistake," the big man apologized. "I should have only wounded him. Poor brainwork on me part there."

"He threatened to cut off my nose and ears, if I didn't do as he told me at the tollhouse," she said softly. "It might not be proper or Christian, but I'm not sorry that he is dead."

Rusty spat a second stream of juice onto the corpse. "Hearing that, I ain't sorry one bit neither."

"What do we do about his body?" Cat asked.

"I'll get a shovel," Reese told her.

"The food won't be getting any better a-sitting in that kettle," Rusty said firmly. "Let's eat first. Mock Doy has no place to go."

"I'm not hungry," Cat spoke up. "If you men don't mind, I'm going back over to the stream and wash."

"That water is colder than a politician's heart!" Rusty said. "And you want to wash?"

"Don't overdo it," Reese added. "Be real easy to catch cold."

Cat did not reply to either of them, but hurried off into the darkness. Soon as she was out of earshot, Rusty looked at Reese.

"Pray tell, what's gotten into the lassie?"

"Durned if I know."

"What did you two do whilst I was playing find-the-peeping-Tom?" he asked. "Must have been good. Old Mock was caught completely by surprise."

"I kissed her."

Rusty grinned. "Say now, sonny!" he teasingly punched Reese on the shoulder hard enough to knock most men tail-over-tin-cup. "I'm proud of you. That there shows some progress!"

"It was a diversion," Reese explained. "She was supposed to fight me off some and then slap me."

"The two of you must have given Mock Doy a purty good show. I got to within about fifteen feet of him before he heard me."

"Yeah, it was convincing."

Rusty squinted suspiciously. "The kissing or the slapping?"

"We didn't get to the slapping."

"No?" His eyes were wide with curiosity. "Tell me, how far did you get, sonny?"

"I told you. We just kissed."

The big man grunted, obviously not convinced. "Aye."

"That's all that happened!" Reese lamented.

CHAPTER 12

WYNGATE FOLLOWED KEATS over to the window. By standing back in the dark interior, they could look out without being seen.

"Claims to be a missionary and his wife," Keats was saying. "You know the word Quan sent about a lawman snooping around. I figured you would want to take a look for yourself."

"I recognize the big fellow, Rusty McCune."

"Yeah, he said they hired him as their guide."

"You believe him?"

Keats chuckled. "I sure wouldn't call him a liar to his face. Man would be one tall mountain to climb, should it come to a fight."

"He could be on the level about his part," Wyngate admitted. "How about the other two?"

"Never seen either of them before. The woman speaks Chinese and translates for her husband."

Wyngate took a forward step, staring hard at the new arrivals. When his eyes rested on the woman, he could not look away.

"By hanna!" he exclaimed. "That is one fine-looking woman."

"She's got a look about her that could melt the lead in your bullets," Keats confirmed. "Ever see such striking blue eyes?"

"You say she can speak Chinese?"

"That's the claim," Keats answered. "The man is a wandering Bible thumper and his wife is his interpreter."

"You think his arrival is a coincidence?"

"Could be, boss. Ain't been no word from Quan since he gave us that warning the other day."

"I want someone to check out the missionary. I'm not taking anyone at face value right now."

"Whatever you say. I'll have one of the boys ride to town and see what they can find out."

"Check with Rusty too. See what he knows about them."

"What about letting them talk to the Chinese?"

"Might not look good to refuse hospitality, in case the pair are telling the truth."

"Tomorrow is Sunday," Keats said. "That works out for a church service of some kind."

"Convenient," he replied thoughtfully. "You tell Bok Fong to handpick fifty or so of the workers. Make sure he instills in their tiny yellow brains that they are to do nothing but listen to the man's sermon and talk religion. One slip and a couple of missionaries are going to have an accident."

"Anything else?"

"Get word to Razor and the Kid to lie low until our visitors are gone. The missionary and his guide might have seen some wanted posters during their travels."

"I doubt that will hurt their feelings," Keats quipped. "They hardly ever leave the joy girls at the tavern. With a couple of evening doves hanging around, the good preacher shouldn't want to get near that place. They ought to be safe enough there."

"Stall our guests for a few minutes while I clear out the back room. We'll show the missionary and his wife proper hospitality and then speed them on their way."

"Then you're going to have them stay in the house with the two of us?"

"We ain't got no place else suitable for a woman." He narrowed his gaze. "Besides, that way we can keep an eye on them."

Keats accepted the explanation and went outside the

house. Wyngate watched through the window, unable to take his eyes off the woman. He felt as if his boots were sunken in lead. There was no strength to move from the spot.

The young lady was clad in a gray dress that reached the ground and buttoned up to her throat. That covering was not enough to hide the fact that she was mature and fully feminine in build. The poke bonnet shaded her face, but did little to hide her marvelous features. Such a face could have belonged to a beautiful child or a nubile young woman. Slightly oval in shape, with a delicate nose, sultry, sculptured lips, and baby-soft cheeks. The eyes were dazzling blue sapphires, brilliant and articulate, ornamented by long, teasing eyelashes.

Wyngate felt his passion rise, simply standing there. What he would not do to have a woman like that for his own.

"She's too good to have some soapbox parson hauling her all over the country and making her old before her time," he said aloud.

The words had a hollow ring within the three-room house. It was enough to get his mind back to the present situation. He reluctantly left the window to clear away enough mess that he could invite guests into the house.

"Best be what he claims," he vowed to himself. "Else, I'm going to have myself that woman, and her man will be lookin' at the underside of six foot of dirt."

Rusty played the part of guide to perfection. He stayed with the horses, insisting that he had to rub them down and groom them personally. When he spoke to Reese, he used a reverent tone of voice and called him Mr. Thompson.

Cat maintained an outward reserve and quietude, offering to answer questions only when asked directly. Lowell Wyngate demonstrated a proper manner when offering them lodging for the night, but his eyes constantly rested on her. When the table was set, Reese was quick to hold the chair for his pretend wife.

"So how long have you been married?" Wyngate directed his question toward Cat. She took a moment to dab at the corner of her mouth with a cloth napkin. It allowed time for Reese to answer the question.

"I met the missus while she was studying Chinese at a mission in San Francisco," he replied. "We found that we had a great deal in common and were married early last year."

If Reese's answering the query annoyed him, Wyngate hid it carefully. He removed his eyes from Cat long enough to regard Reese warily.

"And you say that you are trying to convert the heathen Chinese to our Christian ways?"

"The Good Book says to go forth and preach the word of God," Reese said piously. "I received my calling right after the War Between the States ended."

"Been spreading the Word for several years, have you?"

"Only a short while," Reese told him. "I had to study first under a number of learned ministers. If one doesn't have a church backing them, then much of their missionary work is wasted."

"Why try and bring religion to the Chinese? Most of them are only in this country to make a few dollars. What good will our religion do them back in China?"

"We want to spread the Righteous Word, Mr. Wyngate. I offer them an olive branch that they might plant it both in their hearts and in their homeland. With luck, that branch will grow into a mighty tree that will spread all over the world."

Dorty Keats had been taciturn. Reese recognized him as the kind of man who would take special watching. He was a studier, a man who did not take anything at its surface value. When he spoke, there was an underlying current in his voice, not simple curiosity, but neither outright suspicion.

"You don't look like a man who would take up preaching, Thompson."

"No?"

His gaze was intense, probing for weakness, hedged with distrust. "No."

"And what line of work do you think should be my calling?"

"Maybe a bounty hunter," he said bluntly.

Wyngate laughed, as if Keats had made a joke. "That's my foreman for you." He continued to chuckle. "He don't trust anyone, and he don't believe God ever sticks His nose into the dealings of us mortals."

"Perhaps we could discuss it sometime?" Reese offered.

"Be wasting your breath," Keats replied. "I don't need no holy man praying on my soul. I've done made my bed—I'll sleep in it by myself."

Reese locked gazes with the man. Keats was a closed book, but with a warning on the cover. He would be cold and ruthless in a fight, a hard man to best or kill. Within the depths of Keats's cool, pale-green eyes, Reese recognized a man both capable and deadly.

"If you don't mind a change of subject," Wyngate said shortly, breaking the fixed stare between the two of them, "how did you happen to hire the big ex-trapper for a guide?"

"That was good fortune on my part," Reese answered, swinging his attention back to Wyngate. "It seems that Mr. McCune transported and delivered some gold from one of those tollhouse places. I met him at the bank."

Reese assumed a look of disbelief. "Imagine a man carrying all that money alone," he said, then sighed. "Anyhow, I felt that a man who was so extraordinarily trustworthy was the right man to hire for our trip. He was going to come back up this direction in another week or two for another job, so he agreed to guide us."

"Why to Gold Spur?" Keats anted again.

"There are a number of missions in most any city," Reese responded easily. "I have my destiny to fulfill within the outer regions. One of the poor wretches I met in town said he thought there were a number of Chinese here in the hills."

"Got a name for that wretch?" Keats asked, still openly aggressive and suspicious.

Reese held his calm, but he was growing very tired of the hired man's questioning his every word.

"I detect that you are not only an agnostic, Mr. Keats, but you are the most inquisitive, distrustful man I have met in a long time. What is it you don't like about me?"

"I think you're a faker," he stated flatly.

"Keats!" Wyngate scolded him softly. "That is no way to talk to our guests."

The man relented at once. "Whatever you say, boss."

"Why don't you check the disposition of the men and speak to Bok Fang about the prayer meeting tomorrow?" Wyngate said to Keats.

"Sure thing," he said, pushing back from the table. He paused to tip his head toward Cat. "Ma'am?" he excused himself.

Cat gave him a curt nod, but there was no warmth in her expression. She perfectly demonstrated her displeasure with the subtle motion. Reese made a mental note to tell her how proud he was of her performance.

"Back to you, Mrs. Thompson." Wyngate wasted no time finding an excuse to fawn over Cat again. "Whatever possessed you to learn the Chinese language?"

"My father ran a mission on the edge of China town. I am half Chinese."

"That explains your unique beauty," Wyngate said, displaying a more-than-casual interest in her every word.

"I often helped with the young girls, the ones who were brought into this country to be sold as slaves. To be of any service, I had to learn to speak Chinese."

"What a noble thing to do."

"I'm sure that you don't approve of selling and trading those poor young women," she continued, baiting him.

"Not in the slightest," he was quick to respond. "It's shameless, a real tragedy that such things take place."

"At those disgraceful joy houses, they tell the Chinese girls that we at the mission are witches, that we cut up young girls and feed them to dogs. All manner of lies are used to control the girls and keep them from seeking out help at the missions."

"So you felt that speaking Chinese would help you to put their minds at ease," he deduced. "That makes perfect sense."

She did not respond, but ducked her head slightly in an affirmative nod.

"You were very fortunate to find such a woman as she, Mr. Thompson."

"My most treasured helpmate," Reese replied with some fervor, smiling at the girl. He could not help but notice a flush come into her cheeks.

"I shouldn't wonder." Wyngate continued to devour Cat with his hungry stare.

"Might I ask a simple but perplexing question?" Reese attempted to break his concentration.

"And what would that be?"

"I was wondering about the number of guards you have here. Are the Indians all that active in this part of the country?"

Irritation flashed momentarily across Wyngate's face, but he masked it at once and continued to speak with a mild, congenial tone of voice.

"Indians, bandits, claim jumpers. There ain't no law up

here but the law of the gun, preacher. Takes a small army to hold on to anything worthwhile."

"I understand completely. We have come across a number of ruffians in our travels. It is still a wild and untamed land in many parts of the state."

"Would you care for a bath, Mrs. Thompson?" Wyngate was instantly preoccupied with Cat again. "It would only take a few minutes to heat some water."

"Thank you, but not tonight," she replied carefully. "I'm tired from the long ride. I want nothing but a bed and to sleep till noon."

Wyngate gave her a wide, understanding smile. "We don't have many visitors up this way, but you and your husband are welcome to use the spare room for your stay with us."

"That's very nice of you," she said graciously. "Can I help with any of the cleaning chores?"

"I'll have the cook clear away the dishes," he told her. "As long as you are in my house, you will get nothing but the very best service."

Cat arched her back, stiff from nearly three days in the saddle. When she stood up, both men did likewise.

"Would you excuse me for the night, Mr. Wyngate?"

He made a half-bow toward her. "Certainly, Mrs. Thompson."

She hesitated and looked at Reese. "Are you coming, dear?"

He enjoyed the use of the term of endearment, even if it was in pretense. Rather than risk any suspicion the first night, Reese stretched mightily.

"If our host doesn't mind my turning in early. I am pretty well beat, too." He stepped away from the table. "Besides, I need to be up early to see to the service for the Chinese workers tomorrow. Is there anything I can do to help gather them together?"

"Bok Fong will assemble the congregation," Wyngate

replied. "There is a hollow behind the tavern. That ought to serve your needs."

"You have been a wonderful host, Mr. Wyngate," Reese told him, showing a smile. "I will pray that your business venture here is a success."

Wyngate accepted his comments in silence, unable to keep from watching Cat as she disappeared into the back room. There was visible yearning in his expression, a voracious hunger that transcended envy.

Reese followed after Cat, but hated the feelings that assailed him. He recognized Wyngate's clandestine desire for Cat and was surprised by his own jealousy.

Rusty did not use the corrals for his own animals. He put them on a picket, setting up a night camp back in a stand of pine trees. It did not take any sixth sense to know that he was being watched.

However, Rusty had played cat-and-mouse games for high stakes before. His years in the wilderness had taught him how to trick or slip away from even the wily Apache. It took him only a few casual glances around to pick out two shadowy figures in the darkness.

He cut a sapling and wedged it between the lower branches of two trees. Then he tossed a canvas over the pole and drove a stake in at the four corners and in the middle of both sides. After seeing to the animals, preparing his own meal and having his nightly chew of tobacco, he crawled into the shelter for the night.

Once under the darkness of the canopy, he watched the two spies. Their lack of enthusiasm for the simple task of guarding over a sleeping man was evident soon. One of them got comfortable and wrapped a blanket around his shoulders. Apparently the second man was to have the first watch, but he was so careless that he was smoking a rolled cigarette.

"Shavetails," Rusty grunted in contempt. " 'Tis two sheep they have out there guarding a wolf."

He eased slowly out the back of his tent and took note of the stars. It was unfamiliar country, so he would have to get a fix on his position. Wouldn't do to become lost and not be able to get back into his own camp.

After studying the direction of the dippers, so that he could determine north and south, he picked out a few landmarks that stood out. Clouds were gathering but there was enough moonlight for him to see fairly well. Finally, with the stealth of a gopher snake, he slithered out through the trees and around the rocky hillside.

During his search for a good place to camp, he had noticed several sentry positions and the location of the Chinese tents, the main house, and the tavern. With a mountain man's instincts, he kept away from the main trails and avoided the guards' outposts.

The tavern was ablaze with light. From the only two windows, he could see several men inside, drinking and gambling. A Chinese girl in a red silk blouse and matching bloomers was also in the room.

Rusty crept up next to the dark side of the building and became one of the shadows. For the next hour, he listened to the talk that reached his position. There was little information passed about, until someone new entered the place. As the man's words carried outside, Rusty recognized the voice of Dorty Keats.

"Don't show your faces until it is all clear," Keats was telling someone. "We ain't checked on these missionaries yet, but I don't trust that preacher fella."

"So let's get rid of him," a cool voice responded.

"Boss don't want it that way . . . yet."

"How long we got to hole up here?"

"Tomorrow is Sunday," Keats replied. "Once the holy man spouts his sermon, we'll see that they get on their way. No need taking a chance that they've seen your wanted posters."

"Okay, okay," the first man answered. "We'll keep the girls company until the missionary man and his wife are gone."

Rusty did not listen further, but slinked quietly away from the building. He was not afraid of Keats, but the man was very capable. If anyone was able to spot him in the night, it would be him. There was no need to risk discovery.

A hundred feet up the path, he padded through the sparse brush and rocky formations toward the Chinese village. He circled the huts and made something of a rough count of heads. Then he sought a route that would let him inspect the base of the mountain.

An hour passed, then another. Rusty had been all over the different sides of the broad-back ridge and to the huge mouth of the mountain tunnel. He was working toward his own campsite when he dipped over a swell and down through cavernous terrain. He stepped onto something soft, a peculiar mound of some kind. At first, he thought he had wandered into some kind of diggings in the hollow. As realization dawned, he stopped dead in his tracks.

The wind had picked up. Light rain began to fall and the wet leaves produced a sweet scent, enhancing the smell of freshly turned earth. A distant streak of lightning flashed, throwing a ghostly light over the entire area.

Rusty considered himself a man's man, tough as sun-parched leather. He had buried women and children victims of Indian raids, watched men die, even helped to amputate a limb once. Even so, he hung his head, filled with a sudden and vast emptiness over what he saw. Had he been the slightest bit weaker, he would not have been able to hold back tears.

CHAPTER 13

CAT REMOVED HER dress, but kept on a camisole and full-length petticoat. She reclined on the bed and pulled a single blanket up around her shoulders. With marked embarrassment, she regarded Reese in the dimly lit room.

"You can't sleep on the floor," she said softly. "The bed is plenty big enough for you to sleep next to me."

He recognized the logic of her words: it would arouse suspicion if anyone found they did not share the bed. But to hide his anxiety, Reese put the lamp out before removing his boots and hanging his hat on the bedpost. Since he had been pretending to be a man of God, he wore no gun to be removed.

"Do you think they suspect you?" she asked, breaking the strained silence between them.

Reese sat down on the edge of the bed. "Maybe."

"I don't like the way Mr. Wyngate stares at me," Cat said, still in a hushed voice. "Hoy Quan used to look at me the same way."

"I know what you mean. That miserable lecher practically slobbers with every word he speaks. If I wasn't pretending to be a preacher, I'd close both his eyes for him with some well-placed knuckles."

There was a subtle challenge in her tone of voice. "Why should you want to hit Mr. Wyngate in the eyes?"

Reese cleared his throat and said, "Well . . . to stop him from looking at you the way he has since we arrived. He ain't got a decent bone in his body to blatantly lust after you that way. There's no reason for him to think you would ever show him favor. You're supposed to be married to me."

"And you would stand up for my honor because I am pretending to be your wife?"

"That part makes no difference," he replied. "Every person deserves respect, until they prove otherwise."

"I can't imagine anyone ever fighting for my honor."

He frowned. "Quan wants you, all of those miners, freighters, and travelers wanted you at the tollhouse, and you admit that Wyngate is pining to be your chosen heartthrob. About every man you've come into contact with would fight over you."

"Over me, maybe," she admitted, "but not *for* me."

"Maybe I would only be fighting over you, too. You ever give that any thought?"

"No."

He was stunned by her candor. There had been no hesitation and no doubt in her reply.

"Why not? I'm a man too. I find you a very attractive young woman. What makes you think I'm any different than any of the other men who are chasing after you?"

She did not respond at once. He shifted his weight, pivoting around until he could look into her face. The darkness hid all but a faint outline of her features.

"Well?" he prodded her.

"Because I kissed you," she murmured softly.

"That was only an act to hold Mock Doy's attention," he retorted.

"I was supposed to slap you, remember?"

"Well, uh, Rusty's shot interrupted us. You didn't have time."

"Perhaps . . ." Her voice was only a halting whisper. ". . . Perhaps your memory is not all that good."

Reese discovered that he was holding his breath. "Meaning?"

"You couldn't have—have pretended that well."

"What are you saying, that I'm in love with you?"

"I don't know," she said frankly. "Could you ever love someone of mixed blood?"

Reese leaned toward her until his lips brushed hers. The kiss was tentative at first, cautious and uncertain. He was aware that Cat had never known love in her life, and he now realized that he wanted to give her all his love for the rest of his days.

Quan disliked the arrogant Judge Brown. Cyrus was of the opinion that he was the most important man alive. His wife was an arrogant snob, often speaking out against the Chinese at meetings or in newsletters. He only tolerated Cyrus because of their connection to Wyngate's business deal.

Cyrus showed impatience as Quan extended him the courtesy of offering wine. Yoke Wong came into the room with a serving tray, but the judge angrily waved her away.

"Get rid of the joy girl, Quan!"

"Yoke Wong not joy girl," the woman answered carefully. "Yoke Wong is *ah mah,* is servant."

"Whatever you are, leave us!"

Quan nodded for her to depart. He was careful to keep his anger from showing in his face.

"You risk vely much to come here, Judge."

Cyrus strode over to the curtained door and checked to see that the maid was no longer within earshot. Then he returned his attention to Quan. "Why didn't you tell me there was a lawman snooping around?"

"Quan no think important."

Cyrus snorted his contempt. "You aren't capable of thinking, Quan! I am the one who does the thinking at this end of the business deal."

Quan held his temper. "Why matter? Corbett know nothing. He no guess nothing."

"I heard about his raid at your joy house. What is the matter with you, stealing a white woman? Are you completely crazy or just too stupid to use that simple little brain of yours!"

"She half-Chinese," Quan replied, his teeth clenched to hold his rancor back. "Alley Cat no white."

"So what does the marshal want with her?"

"No can say."

Cyrus paced briskly about the room. "I don't like the way this is going, Quan. I have put my shipping business at risk. Everything I own is wrapped up in financing that gold-mine operation."

"Same for me," Quan told him.

"Four men working to provide capital for the tunnel were killed the other day. That lawman was in on that. Too much is starting to go wrong. Do you know where the marshal is now?"

"He go away."

"Do you have anyone following him?"

"Mock Doy."

"Well, a rider from Wyngate told one of my informants at the tollhouse that a man claiming to be a missionary arrived up there to preach the gospel to the Chinese." He glared at Quan. "He was traveling with a young wife who translates for him!"

"Alley Cat." Quan breathed the name.

"If so, your Mock Doy is probably dead. Our four hold-up specialists are dead. A United States marshal is up at Snake Canyon, and you don't *think* I ought to be kept informed!"

Quan had nothing to say to that. He was not surprised that Mock had failed to kill Corbett, but how did Corbett know to go to Snake Canyon?

"Well, I'm cutting myself a lifeline, Quan." Cyrus was red-faced, enraged that nothing had worked out. "You and Wyngate can find your own raft, but I won't drown with you. That marshal was snooping in the records office, but I have access to those. I can get my name removed from those mining claims. By the time I'm finished, I won't have any ties with either of you."

"And what of you and me agreement? How do I bring more labor gangs from Hong Kong?"

"You and I are no longer engaged in the labor-import business, Quan. Find yourself another partner." He stomped toward the door, but paused, glowering back at him.

"You yellow-skinned pigtails are a blight on this country, Quan. I hope all of your kind are shipped back to China!"

The door slammed, throwing the room into silence. Quan's fleshy hands were knotted into fists. He snatched up a glass of *woo ga pai* and took a big swallow. The rice brandy burned down his throat and made his eyes water, but it did not slake his rage.

"What is your order?" Ti Kong had entered the room without making a sound.

"You heard?"

"No man alive is to speak to you in such a way," Ti replied, his voice as cold as chipped ice. "Say the word and I will deal with him. A bullet would not be traced to the Chinese district," Ti promised. "In his effort to save himself, he will probably add to the evidence against you. Every moment he lives is a danger to you."

"When could you do this thing?"

"Not until the darkness of night covers my movement into the white part of the city."

"I know you are capable, Ti Kong. Be like a shadow and move like the night breeze. Let us be rid of Cyrus Brown and his bigotry once and for all."

The leader of Quan's fighting tongs showed a rare smile. "It shall be a favorite memory until my last day of life. I will not fail you."

Sunday, several of the rough characters who stood guard about the camp and trails came to Reese's service. Among those in attendance, he noticed a familiar face, but could not readily place it. The Chinese men were gathered together into an audience of nearly fifty souls. They were perfectly quiet and attentive, and offered not a word between them. They sat on the ground in a semicircle, while Reese read the Sermon on the Mount from the Bible. After the reading he did not try to preach, but rather told them only of the love Jesus had for all men.

Cat was an able interpreter, but often had to pause for the right words. If anything the men heard went to heart, it did not show in their faces. They were a crowd of human scarecrows: weary, gaunt, hollow-faced. Only when she brought out a bag of litchis and passed them out did the men show gratitude.

Reese moved through the group and shook hands with many of them. He took note of the scarred and callused hands from their arduous labor. There were several scars that could have been inflicted from a whip. Not one of the white men stayed to speak to him, leaving before he began to meet the Chinese individually.

All the while, a slender, weasel-faced Chinese watched every move that was made. Bok Fong, the laborers' head man, was careful to always stay within hearing distance of Cat, but far enough away from Reese that he could not be questioned himself.

Rusty appeared toward the end of the service. He looked anxious, but did not attempt to make contact.

Reese noticed him, but the opportunity to speak did not present itself. Dorty Keats showed up and Rusty ambled off toward his camp. Reese decided that he would have to sneak out that night and meet up with him.

"How'd the meeting go, preacher?" Keats asked Reese, showing little real interest.

"Not the most lively congregation I've ever encountered," he replied.

"These boys put in six twelve-hour shifts a week. I reckon they're too tired to do much talking."

"I suppose you have a point there."

"Boss wanted me to invite you to stick around for the night. Ain't much sense in pulling out this late in the day."

"That would suit us fine. An early start tomorrow sounds good."

"We don't usually have much of a lunch, but our Chinese cook is fixing a nice meal for tonight."

"Again, you have our thanks." Reese was cordial. "Would you mind if we went down to the Chinese village and called upon any of the sick or injured?"

"Don't have any," Keats replied. "One of the boys get hurt or sick, we send them to Grayson's place. His wife is something of a medico. She either gives them something, treats the injury, or ships them by stage to the nearest real hospital."

"That's very humane."

"Besides that, most of them Chinese treat their own problems. Bok Fong has snake wine, dried sea horses, toads, and ground deer horns as remedies." He pulled a face. "Wouldn't catch me sticking anything like that into my mouth, but he keeps them going."

Reese was wise enough not to mention going into the Chinese living compound again. The huts were off in the distance, crowded together like Indian wickiups. He let the matter drop.

Keats appeared outwardly friendly, but a light frost had crept into his eyes. Reese had the eerie feeling that he was one very dangerous man.

"Have fun, preacher. I'll tell the boss that you're sticking around for one more night."

Reese watched the gunman walk slowly over the small rise until he was out of sight. A prickling ran down his neck, but he shook it off. He had a job to do.

CHAPTER 14

AS DARKNESS COVERED the city of San Francisco, the street lamps in the richer part of town were lit. There were few lights showing in the poor districts or down the back alleys.

Ti Kong carried a Navy Colt in his belt as he made his way from one section of town to the next. Part of the shadows, he quickly crossed past any open ground, avoided all lighted areas. He was a ghost in the night, working the back streets, wary of anyone who was moving about.

Reaching the fine large houses, he took even more time and precautions. He prudently checked each yard for dogs that might bark, sometimes going a block around a possibly noisy mutt. When he came upon Judge Brown's house, he did not approach it at once. Instead, he remained deep in the shadows and watched for his chance.

The garbage piled at the corner of an alley was a safe place to wait, as people naturally gave it wide berth. Someone had dumped some spoiled potatoes, and the odor was particularly offensive.

It took an hour before Ti was certain that only Judge Brown and his wife were home. Their servants did not share the living quarters in the main house; that would have been unsatisfactory for the haughty woman of the house. She was content to have Mexicans clean her house and cook her meals, but they were not allowed to sleep under the same roof with her.

Ti wondered what would happen to the woman, once her husband was no longer there to give her everything she demanded. The judge claimed to have put all of his money behind the gold-mine deal. How laughable if she wound up broke and destitute. What an appropriate fate, should she end her years working as a servant for someone else, cleaning up after them!

The judge's wife finally went to the back of the house. Ti figured that was the location of the bedroom. Judge Brown stepped out into the evening air, standing with the light behind him. He bit the end off a long cigar and stuck it between his lips. Apparently Mrs. Brown did not let him smell up the house with the foul smoke from the cigar.

Even his manner of smoking seemed pompous, as if he were a man of great importance. He regularly treated the Chinese, the Mexicans, and the whites in the poor districts with disdain. Tonight a small cloud of smoke rose from his pursed lips.

With catlike grace, Ti sprang over the mound of trash. He crept through the shadows until he was only fifteen feet from the front door of Judge Brown's house. A quick look around told him no one else was in sight. He pulled the gun and eased the hammer back on the trigger. As Cyrus put the cigar between his teeth, Ti took careful aim and squeezed the trigger.

The report sounded like a cannon, echoing in the stillness of the night. Before the smoke could rise from the muzzle, before Judge Brown could comprehend that a lead missile had penetrated his heart, Ti was gone.

Shouts were raised far behind him. A scream was heard. Ti stuck deep within the shadows, a silent, undetectable phantom. Quickly Ti reached the poorer neighborhoods, where he slowed his pace, watchful that no one should spot him.

Entering Wyngate's house, Reese was caught completely by surprise. A fist slammed into the side of his face and knocked him into the wall. Before he could get his wits about him, another blow jarred his teeth.

Cat yelled something, but Reese did not hear what she said. He instinctively covered up, lifting his fists even with his head. That got the wind driven from him, as another knotted fist landed hard against his stomach. He grunted from the blow, realizing that his attacker was a fairly large man.

Dazed, he saw the assailant draw back for another roundhouse punch. Reese could not suck any air into his lungs, but he did manage to duck away from the man's next swing. In almost the same dodge, he lashed out with a countering right hand and clipped the man above his left eye.

"Get him, Swede!" Keats's voice encouraged Reese's opponent.

"Take him apart!" Wyngate added.

Reese had been so unprepared to fight, he had virtually no chance. A bone-jarring fist rocked his head again, then two more jolts punished his midsection. He staggered blindly while he took the severe pounding. His own reaction had been too slow, and his countering punches packed no real power. He scored a number of times, but the Swede was like a bull. He shook off the feeble jabs and kept hammering away until Reese slumped to the floor.

"That's good!" Wyngate ordered. "Don't want him dead just yet."

"By gume! I done give him vot for."

"Sure did, Swede. Check him for any hidden weapons."

"Vat he teenk, dat I don't know da man vot outbid me fer da voman? I knowed dem both. I did, by golly!"

Reese was breathing hard, dizzy and barely conscious, suffering from the painful beating. As hands went through his pockets and patted him down, he could taste sweet, salty blood in his mouth. There was a throbbing above one eye and a warm trickle of blood ran down along his cheek. His lips felt twice their normal size, and his ribs ached with every breath. The Swede had worked him over pretty good.

"So, you're the same girl that was taken from Grayson's Tollhouse." Wyngate turned his attention to Cat. "I wondered about there being more than one half-Chinese girl around."

"I'll bet a month's pay that our preacher here is the lawman," Keats spoke up.

Wyngate pounded Swede on the back. "We owe you a favor."

"By gume, she don' look da same, dressed up like dat," the Swede noted. "But I never forget dem eyes of hers. No sir, I never forget dem."

"Thanks for the help, Swede," Wyngate told him. "You did just fine."

"She does durn-near look like a white woman," Keats said. "Talks without any accent at all."

"She's all dressed up like one too," Wyngate joined in. "Imagine her nerve, trying to act the part of a real lady." His voice became cruel. "Alley Cat, the half-chink from the gutters of Chinatown."

"I done offered more dan four hun'red dollars fer her," the Swede volunteered. "Vot about dat, Mr. Vyngate. Do I gets to take her vith me?"

"Not just yet, Swede," Wyngate replied. "You round up a couple of the boys and bring Rusty McCune up to join our little party. I don't know if he's mixed up with this character or not, but we'll soon find out."

"By golly, I vill bring him," Swede promised. "He not be so tough."

A rough hand took hold of Reese's hair and yanked his head back. He could see clearly through only one eye. The other one was swollen shut. Keats was standing over him.

"So are you a marshal?" he demanded. "Why come all the way up here to Snake Canyon? What are you looking for?"

"I came to preach to the heathen Chinese," Reese muttered through swollen lips. "What is the matter with that?"

"Sure, and all preachers go around shelling out five hundred bucks for a joy girl and then steal her from her rightful owner."

"Some of Quan's tong took back the girl, after you sneaked away from Grayson's. Yet she's with you again. How did you manage that?" Wyngate asked.

"I took her away from Quan," Reese replied. "I married her to prevent anyone from trying to enslave her again."

Wyngate snickered at his lie. "You tell a tall tale, Thompson, or whatever your name is, but your story don't hold water."

"Let's kill him, to be on the safe side," Keats suggested. "I don't trust him one bit."

Wyngate hesitated. "Not until we know what he is up to."

"What do we do with him then?"

"Put a rope around his neck and give him a ride back of your horse, Keats." Wyngate smiled, a wicked light dancing in his eyes. "Once he has been peeled like a potato, his tongue might loosen some. Meanwhile, I'll question the lady. I know she'll want to cooperate with us."

"Whatever you say, boss."

Reese's heart dropped to the pit of his stomach. Keats half lifted and half dragged him outside. Reese was shoved to the ground and tasted a mouthful of dirt.

A rope was slipped over his head and jerked tight. He grabbed on to it, to stop it from choking him. Even as he managed to get his fingers inside the noose to protect his neck, the other end was pulled taut.

Reese felt the rope yanked until it nearly cut through his windpipe. If he hadn't had his fingers laced around the noose, it would have strangled him.

The ground tore and hammered at his body. He was blinded by the dust from the horse's hooves. He bounced crazily along the ground, twisting and turning, rolling over and over. The world was a blur of spinning and whirling images, filled with sharp rocks and brutal clumps of brush. He did his best to keep his head up and rolled away from huge boulders or small trees that would have broken his bones. Even so, his body was pulverized by the rough ground.

The jerking motion finally stopped, and Reese gasped for breath. He pulled at the rope to loosen it enough to get air into his burning lungs. His throat felt crushed and his fingers were numb and bleeding.

"How's the ride back there?" Keats taunted him.

With all his effort, Reese shoved the rope up over his head. Then he rolled onto his back and suffered the anguish of a thousand scrapes, cuts, and bruises. Everything from his toenails to the last strand of hair on his head hurt.

"Know what raw ground meat feels like," he barely whispered through the dust that coated his throat.

"You're a game gent," Keats said, approaching him. "That little ride would have killed most men."

Reese ran his tongue over his puffy, bleeding lips. "You mean I ain't dead?"

"Another trip around the top of the hill and you will be, ace. Why not tell me why you're here. We know you're that marshal the highbinders sent for."

Reese saw no need to lie about it. After all, they knew who Cat and Rusty were. With a little luck, he might at least convince Keats that the others knew nothing.

"Reese Corbett," he said, sighing. "I hired the girl to help me. I didn't think anyone would suspect her if I passed her off as my wife."

"And Rusty?"

"Never met him before he saved my hide below Grayson's place. He kept those boys from beating me to death.

I convinced him that I was a missionary and hired him as a guide."

"Well, Swede and a couple of the boys will check that story."

"What difference does it make who I am?"

"Why did you come up here?" he asked.

"Looking for some missing Chinese. I guess I found them, huh?"

Keats laughed. "Did you? Good work . . . too bad you won't get to tell anybody."

"Why kidnap them?" he asked.

"The coal miners have a union, Corbett. They get four dollars a day in the hole. Even if we put the Chinese on at half that, it would have cost us ten thousand a month for labor. We ain't set up like the railroad. The government don't help us finance our operation."

"And so you forced slave labor?"

"We've been hammering away and blowing chips out of the Old Maid for better'n six months. Even when we have the nitroglycerin we need, it is a good day that manages two feet. We're barely to the halfway point, and we've spent five hundred thousand dollars on that stubborn monster."

"Free labor must cut down on expenses a lot," Reese said sarcastically.

"Still have to pay the guards and buy food and supplies. Them Chinese live as cheap as anyone alive, but they still eat."

"With Quan and Cyrus Brown backing you, I would think you could get by without slave labor."

"How'd you know about the judge?"

"I did a little investigating."

"Then you ought to know that the kind of money we're talking ain't exactly bread crumbs. That sizable investment has about broke them both."

"For a piece of gold mine?" Reese could not believe it. "They risked that kind of money on a dream?"

"We took samples that showed good color. There must be a dozen mines back here that will equal the Comstock Lode. All we need is a tunnel so we can ship the ore."

"You're all crazy."

"Kind words ain't going to save what's left of you, Corbett. We'd better see what the boss wants to do with you. Get on your feet."

Reese made an effort to rise, then slumped back down. He shook his head from side to side.

"Think something is broken, Keats," he said, grimacing from the pain. "I can't feel my legs."

The gunman took a moment to consider his options. Then he shook out the length of rope and tied Reese right there on the ground. He stepped back and said, "There . . . that should hold you until I get back."

"You're real handy with ropes, Keats," he said hoarsely. "Hope we can turn the tables sometime."

Keats kicked dirt in Reese's face, turned, and walked away.

CHAPTER 15

REESE TESTED HIS bonds, but Keats had tied him securely. Being so battered up, he was fortunate to be conscious. Desperation seized him, but he was helpless. Once Wyngate decided that he had told them all he knew, he would likely be dumped over a cliff or buried in the nearest hole.

Even as a foreboding of doom weighed down on him like a foot-deep blanket of sand, a swarthy form appeared out of the darkness. Reese blinked and squinted through his swollen eyes, trying to make out the bulky shadow.

"By all the saints, sonny!" Rusty's hushed voice was like sweet music to his ears. "What have you gotten yourself into?"

"Quick!" Reese whispered. "They sent some men down to round you up. They're onto me!"

Rusty pulled out his skinning knife and knelt down at Reese's side. "Aye, I crossed the path of them fellers," he said nonchalantly. "A big Swede and another varmint."

Reese turned his head, trying to look around. "What happened to them?"

"Mind the blood." Rusty referred to the knife in his hand. "Blade's still sharp enough to cut these here ropes."

"You killed them both?"

"Seemed the thing to do," the big man replied. "He not be a coward, that there Swede. Got to hand him that. He could have run off when I took them from behind and rid myself of the other one. But he pulled his own knife and we had a go." Rusty lifted his left arm to show a crudely wrapped bloody bandage. "He come close."

Reese shook off the bindings, but he was already grow-

135

ing stiff from the pounding his body had taken. When he sat up, the world spun around in front of his eyes.

"You want me to carry you?"

"Got to get Cat out."

Rusty gave his head a negative shake. "No chance right now, sonny. While you and Keats were enjoying your game of skin-the-marshal, two other fellows went to the house. I'm thinking the guards check in regular with the boss. Both of them looked as if they could trade bites wth a Texas rattler and come out ahead."

"We'll have to think of *something*."

Reese used the big man's help to get to his feet. His legs were bruised and bleeding, but he was still able to walk. "Let's get out of sight, first off. Keats will be back at any minute."

"Come with me."

"Where to?"

"Got something to show you," Rusty told him. "After that, I think we is going to have us a time staying alive."

Reese kept up as best he could, but every muscle ached. His neck burned from the rope, his arms were scraped and raw, knees, chest, and back all bleeding in a dozen places. His clothes were little more than tattered rags, soaked with blood.

Rusty led the way through a stand of trees, along a brush-shrouded landscape, then along a narrow wash. When they broke out into an open glen, Reese staggered to a stop. It took him a few seconds to penetrate the dusk enough to see the rows and rows of mounds and flat wooden stakes.

"I counted them last night." Rusty's voice was gravely reverent. "There be sixty-eight."

Reese's mind was no longer on his injuries. He suffered a wave of anguish and a great emptiness filled his chest. "Sixty-eight graves?"

"Them there little markers all have Chinese scribble on

them. I'd say that the writing lists the name of the man buried there."

"Good Lord, Rusty!" Reese exclaimed. "I don't think that many Chinese died during the entire laying of the Continental Railroad!"

"Six months of work—that would be about eleven of them every month."

"No wonder they had to hire hard cases to guard them."

"I went to the tunnel and about the Chinese camp, Corbett. I figure there are about two hundred altogether."

"That isn't a tunnel, it's a tomb!"

"So what do we do?" Rusty asked. "You're the law, sonny."

Reese looked over the numerous rows of graves. Sixty-eight lives lost. Sixty-eight men, whose hopes and dreams would never be realized.

"Do you have an extra gun?"

"I stowed away your rifle and have the two guns I took from Swede and that other fellow. Sonny, it might be wise for me to point out that we are still looking at long odds."

"Did you get a count of the guards?"

"Figure eight or nine, besides Keats and Wyngate," he answered. "But there are another two or three at the tavern. That means no less than a dozen."

"You told me that you could take any ten men," Reese reminded him. "Don't tell me you were only bragging."

Rusty's chest expanded with indignation. "With me fists, I'd take on all of them, sonny. Guns is something different. A man can only shoot one direction at a time." He thought of something. "Maybe we could get past the outpost, there at the pass, and you could bring in the army?"

"They could cover everything up before we could get help. Besides that, I don't want to leave Cathy behind."

"We'll need to be doing something right quick, or else they might decide to use her to force us to surrender. I wouldn't rule that out with this sort of varmints."

"Where do the guards stay when they are not on duty?"

"A couple shacks down by the tavern. I was down there listening to chatter last night. I heard them tell a couple of bandits to stay low until you were gone."

"What else did you learn?"

"The one shack is for someone called the Chemist. He uses it for his work and storage. The other is mostly bunks for the guards."

"Anything in that storage shed that we could use?"

Rusty grinned his wide smile. "One fellow happened to mention that they had a full store of nitroglycerin for blasting."

Reese did some quick thinking. "I need to swap clothes and pick up a gun. Then I think we ought to pay a visit to that storage shed."

" 'Tis with you I am."

"Aye," he used Rusty's familiar reply. Then he spoke in a voice that was as hard and cold as a January morning in Montana. "We are going to put Wyngate out of business."

Cat sat in despondent silence, unable to think of anything but the pain and suffering Reese was enduring. She experienced horrible dread at the thought of him being killed. She did not look up or respond to any of Wyngate's questions. His voice was raised in anger, but she ignored him.

His rage was diverted by the arrival of two men. They were from a guard post and did not have much to report, but almost immediately Keats returned. As he entered the house, she risked a fleeting glance past him, hoping against all odds to see Reese.

"Got him trussed up like a calf for branding, boss," Keats said, gloating. "Took him for quite a ride."

"He talk?"

"Admitted that he was a marshal. Also said he hired the girl to speak Chinese for him and pretend to be his wife."

"What about Rusty?"

"Claimed to have hired him as a guide. Didn't sound like he told him nothing about his plan."

"So the preacher turned out to be a marshal?" the one guard spoke up. "Sounds like your gold mine ain't going to ever produce nothing, Wyngate. I'm wondering if we all are wasting our time up here."

"The marshal don't have any evidence of anything," Wyngate replied. "If he meets with an accident, no one will be the wiser."

"What about the other two?" Keats wanted to know. "Can't let the girl here go flapping her lips over the country."

"She's staying here," Wyngate told him. "So far, she hasn't decided if she will become my housekeeper or if she wants to serve some time as a joy girl."

"How about Rusty McCune?" Keats asked. "Hate to kill him for being nothing more than a guide."

"Can't be helped. He knows about us up here, and he brought the marshal to us. I don't see how we can let him go."

"I'll do the chore," the one guard said, his voice strangely gruff. "He helped to kill the three Vougal brothers. I'd say it's time to pay him back for that."

"That had slipped my mind," Wyngate admitted. "That payroll he was carrying should have been ours. We lost some good boys at his hands."

There was a knock at the door. Then, without waiting for anyone to answer, a man came bursting into the room.

"Skyler and Swede are both dead!" he announced excitedly. "Found them down by that guide's camp."

"Any sign of Rusty?"

"No."

"Untie the man outside and help bring him into the house. No need to take a chance on losing him."

The man frowned. "Ain't no one outside."

Keats leapt to the doorway and stared out into the dark. He cursed under his breath.

"He told me that he couldn't feel his legs. I tied him up good, but he's gone."

"Rusty McCune," Wyngate concluded for them all. "He is more than just a hired guide."

"So it seems, boss. Now what?"

"Send word to the boys at the pass. Then round up the rest of our men. We'll organize two groups to search for the marshal and his pal. There are only so many places they can hide. No one can get off this mountain without using the main trail."

"We could take the girl here and use her for bait," Keats suggested. "We could strip her bare and drag her back of a horse. If we hanged her by her hair from the nearest tree, they'd both up and surrender."

Cat's heart stopped. She suddenly lost the power even to breathe. To her relief, Wyngate did not approve of that plan of action. His voice was calm and objective. "What makes you think the marshal cares anything for the girl? She's half-Chinese."

"She don't look it," the one guard replied.

"I'll do whatever it takes to get those two," Wyngate vowed. "But I'll hold the girl for a reserve measure. If the marshal wants her, he is likely to try and rescue her. If not, we wouldn't gain anything by torturing her."

"Whatever you say," Keats gave in easily.

Cat flicked a glance at him. His words were patronizing, without conviction. She had a terrible feeling about him. He was not just coldhearted like Wyngate, he was a man with ice crystals in his blood. Of all the men in the room, he was the one she feared most.

Wyngate took hold of her arm. "Come on, Alley Cat." She did not resist, going with him into the bedroom.

There was no window and only the one door. As he led

her inside the room, he spun her about. She looked up and found his face livid, eyes filled with desperate desire.

"I could let Keats have his way," he muttered through clinched teeth. "You'd better think about treating me good. If I give the word, you'll be hanging naked from a tree!"

"It's no wonder you are so desperate to find gold. Any woman you want, you'll have to buy!" she said boldly.

His hand flashed in front of her eyes and the sting of a slap rocked her head. She shut her eyes to hold back the tears.

"I'm not a patient man, Alley Cat," he said, sneering, his breath in her face. "You'd best think about your choices up here. You be nice to me and I'll let you be the lady of this house. No one else will touch you. When we start taking millions in gold out of the mountain, I'll buy you nice clothes and jewelry. You will want for nothing."

Cat blinked back the moisture in her eyes, the smarting sensation still very real from her ear to her lower jaw. Wyngate had used an open palm, but he had struck her quite hard.

"Think about it," he told her again. "You give me trouble and you'll not only serve my needs, but you'll end up in the tavern, working as a joy girl. You want to have men like Razor Back Jeeters and the Albino Kid pawing you all night?"

She did not respond, her emotions under tight rein. So long as Reese was alive, she would cling to the hope that he would somehow manage to save her. If they killed him, she would rather die than give in to Wyngate. She knew that she loved Reese, and life without him would be an empty existence. She would wait and pray and hope.

CHAPTER 16

REESE KEPT MOVING, afraid he would become too stiff to walk should he pause to sit down and rest. He picked up a different shirt and trousers from a clothesline and changed out of his bloody rags. When they reached the face of the Old Maid, Rusty left Reese at the base and did some reconnaissance. He returned a few minutes later.

"So much for Sunday being a day of rest," Rusty told him first thing. "The night crew be working. Must be sixty men at the end of the tunnel."

"So now what?"

"I spied their stash of explosives, lad," Rusty said, winking meaningfully. "I'd guess that there be two hundred barrels of blasting powder stacked inside the opening."

"Any guards?"

"That one Chinaman who was doing some interpreting, Bok Fang or Fong, something like that."

"I know the one."

"I've an idea for shutting down this operation," Reese said. "You game for taking another risk?"

"You talk, I'll listen."

Reese kept watch for a time, until Rusty gave him the ready signal. Then Reese moved out into plain sight and walked toward the crew. Bok Fong was startled to see him and his feet were suddenly nailed to the ground. His eyes grew as round and wide as silver dollars.

"What you want?" he demanded.

"Get everyone out of here, Fong," Reese warned him shortly. "I won't tell you twice."

"No!" he shouted. "You no belong here. You go!"

Reese pulled his gun and took aim at the man. "You refusing to get them out, Fong?"

"We go! We go!" he instantly reversed that decision. "We go!"

The man began shouting in his native language. The workers were confused at first, but then dropped their picks, shovels, and drills and ran for the exit. Reese followed along after them, to make certain that every man ahead of him was out. He had doused the lamps toward the exit, to hide his movements from the camp.

Rusty stood at the dark entrance, ready to carry out the plan. As the Chinese continued to retreat toward their village, he handed a match to Reese.

"Think it will work?"

"A hundred or more kegs of black powder and fifteen quarts of nitro, sonny. I be a-thinking that if it don't bring the house down, it ought to at least crack some plaster."

"Think you can get us three horses? When this goes up, I'll have to grab Cat during the confusion and make a run for it."

" 'Tis a fight we'll have getting past that outpost at the edge of the cliff trail."

"Better odds than taking on the entire dozen men."

"I'll swipe broncs for the three of us and meet you at the main house. If they haven't killed us by that time, perhaps we'll have us a chance."

Reese stuck out his hand. "Whatever happens, Rusty McCune, I want you to know that I consider you the best friend I ever had."

The big man gripped his hand in a firm shake and smiled, showing his teeth in his usual manner. "I'm betting there is worse things to get killed over than that."

"See you at the house."

"Thirty seconds is what you'll be having with that fuse," Rusty replied. "That give you enough time to make it?"

"I'll make it."

The Irishman hurried off into the darkness. Reese estimated that Rusty would need no less than fifteen minutes to gather the horses. Bok Fong was sure to run and get help. The tavern was far closer than Wyngate's house. He was likely to come back with several men at any moment.

He didn't like their odds of escaping, but then they had been lucky so far to be alive. Riding past that guard post was going to be like charging into the teeth of a full-blown tornado. It was unrealistic to think that all three of them would get past unscathed. If only he could think of a better plan of action. If he had more time . . .

The sound of approaching steps alerted Reese. He ducked into the mouth of the tunnel and backed up against the smooth rock wall. Drawing his gun, he held his breath and watched.

There were three men. Two had their guns out, and the third was a Chinese. He recognized Bok Fong first, then felt his stomach twist into knots. As he stared to penetrate the night, he saw that the other two were none other than Razor Back Jeeters and the Albino Kid!

"You taking us on a wild-goose chase or something, Fong?" the Kid wanted to know.

"No, no!" he said excitedly. "You come, you see. Is no wild goose, is crazy man—make workers run away."

"Don't see anything down the tunnel but your lamps."

"No!" Fong maintained. "Crazy man, he there!"

Reese remained dead still, not breathing, not moving even an eyelash, as the three men walked past him. Why would a couple of crazed bandits be tied in with a shady mining operation? He had to wonder if the four ambushers he and Rusty had killed had not also been mixed up with Wyngate. Thieves, killers, kidnappers, a judge—the promise of gold had sealed some very unusual relationships.

He gripped his pistol and fought for self-control as he watched the men who had shot up Silver Thorn, leaving five people shot down and a child crippled for life.

"Hold it right there!" he shouted. "Drop your guns or die!"

The two killers did not even hesitate. They both turned as one, shooting blindly behind them. Bok cried out in terror. He attempted to run, but Razor shot him point blank. Before he could even fall, Razor jerked the man's body over to use as a shield.

Reese scrambled back out the entrance. He fired back at the dark, undefined figures, but the two men had backed deep into the shadows. He could not get a good shot at them.

Bullets screamed off of the walls and whistled past him. Reese avoided getting near the wall of stacked powder, but took up a position that covered the entire entrance into the tunnel.

"Give it up, Razor!" he shouted. "I've got a hundred barrels of black powder ready to blow this cave down around your ears."

They answered him with another round of shots. Reese had no choice. He was running out of time. The guards from all over the plateau would be drawn to the gunfire. He had to get away or risk having no chance to rescue Cat and make good an escape.

Even as bullets kicked up around him, Reese stuck a match to the fuse. Then he scrambled back a few feet and waited, his gun ready. He expected Razor and the Albino to try to make a break for safety. Instead, they moved deeper into the tunnel.

"You want us," Razor yelled, "you come and get us!"

Reese gave the fuse an anxious look. It was more than halfway to the kegs. He had no more time for talk. The fate of the two killers was sealed. They were too deep into the tunnel to ever get out in time.

Spinning about, Reese ran away from the entrance. His legs were battered and sore, but his muscles responded to the dangerous situation. He got a hundred yards before a tremendous concussion rocked the earth. The force of the blast knocked him off his feet.

Rocks, grit, and debris flew in all directions. A chain reaction was started by the powder, as each quart of nitro went off simultaneously. The result was a seemingly endless blast that made the mountain tremble and shake violently.

Rock slides crashed down from the Old Maid. It was as if she had been holding her skirt and petticoats up to her knees, then let them all fall at one time. Earth, rock, and clouds of dust and smoke billowed so thick that they blacked out the sky.

Reese coughed from the inhalation of dust and squinted through the nebulous haze that covered the land. Then he was up and moving, skirting high ground, making his way quietly through brush and around outcropping rocks. The house came into sight as he heard men's alarmed voices.

He could see shadows moving near the house. As Reese suspected, most of the hired men ran toward the tunnel entrance to see what had happened.

Clear of the major cloud that was settling to the ground, Reese took a few deep breaths to regain his stamina. Keeping his eyes moving, he tried to stay aware of everything that was happening. Once he was certain that most of the hired men had left their positions, he streaked from his place of concealment and slid to a stop at the doorway of the house. He had only a split second to react, ready to fire instantly.

Keats and Wyngate were both in the room. Cat was not in sight. Keats had the reaction of a surprised cat, spinning, clawing for his gun.

Without hesitation, Reese pulled the trigger of his gun. Once . . . twice . . . three times.

Keats staggered from each bullet's impact but still managed to fire back blindly.

One slug chipped the door casing, then Reese felt something burn along his ribs, a white-hot streak that backed him up a step. He put another round into the die-hard gunman.

Wyngate charged at a window and dove through. Reese managed one hasty shot his direction, but knew he had missed. He escaped into the night.

Holding a hand against his injured ribs, Reese hurried toward the back room. He shoved the door open, but Cat was not there. Instead, there was a hole in the wall where someone had removed several boards.

Reese came back out and paused to look down at the dying man on the floor. Keeping his empty gun trained on Keats, he knelt down over him.

Keats was on his back, his breathing ragged, eyes pinched from the pain. Even as Reese appeared before his eyes, he grit his teeth.

"Knew . . . knew we shoulda kilt you right . . . right off," he gasped before drawing his final breath. Then his eyes stared blindly into space.

Reese wasted no more time, quickly stepping over the body. He took up a position at the door, confounded at not finding the girl. Staring out into the dark, he tried to think.

"Where are you, Rusty?" he said to himself. "Wyngate will have every gun in the place down on us!"

Even as the thought crossed his mind, several men came toward the cabin. Reese readied his gun, quickly taking a few moments to reload.

"Keats!" one of them called. "What's going on? Why the shooting?"

"Everything is going to hell around here!" another

growled. "The whole mountain blows up, shooting coming from everywhere, and ain't no one around. I don't like it."

"This is United States Deputy Marshal Reese Corbett!" he announced boldly. "This gold-mine project is closed. There'll be no more paydays at Gold Spur!"

The men spread out and took cover. Reese counted at least six. He was surrounded, inside a building that had two windows, a door, and a hole in the back room big enough for a grown man to come through. Realistically, he was a trapped animal waiting for the final blow.

"Where is Wyngate?" one of the men asked.

"He ran like a scalded banshee!" Reese replied. "Keats is dead at my feet, and both Razor Back and the Albino Kid were killed in the explosion. A posse is on its way and all of you are under arrest."

There was some discussion, as the men were moving to better positions. Reese knew he had virtually no chance of holding off so many men. He backed up far enough to blow out the room's only lamp, then moved quickly into a dark corner.

"To heck with this!" one man said sourly. "He's right about one thing—no Wyngate, no more paydays. I'm not sticking around here until a whole company of marshals ride in."

Before the others could decide whether to fight or run, a great number of shadows appeared on the horizon.

"This here be Rusty McCune!" the big Irishman's voice boomed in the night. "If you boys wish to stick it out, you'll be a-knowing that I'm with the United States marshal. Along with him and me, there's two hundred armed Chinese workers ready to whip your butts!"

"I'm getting out!" a man exclaimed.

"I'm with you!" another spoke up. "I ain't getting paid to be chopped into pieces by a hundred Chinese!"

The henchmen scampered about, all going different

directions. Within seconds, there was not a gunman in sight.

Rusty led the way forward, followed closely by Cat and a mob of Chinese.

"I thought I sent you to get us some horses!" Reese said, relieved to see them both safe.

"Got lost in the dark." Rusty grinned. "I decided to bust Cathy out first. When the explosion shook the mountain, I tore off a couple of boards. She squirmed through like a wee mouse and we did us the old hotfoot down to the Chinese camp to round up some help."

Cat came closer, peering hard at Reese in the dark. "You've been shot!"

"Probably a relief to him, after the other beatings he's been getting this night," Rusty said.

"Come sit down and let me get a look at it," she directed. "Light a lamp, Rusty."

"What'll I be a-doing about our army?" Rusty asked.

Cat spoke to them shortly and the entire group hurried away. As Reese sat down on a chair, she began to unbutton his shirt.

"What'd you tell them?"

"That we start for home tomorrow morning. They are going to pack, make litters for the injured or sick, and be ready to march at sunup."

"Might have them throw together an extra litter for me. I'm about done in."

The lamp threw a soft light throughout the room. Rusty tapped his gun. "Methinks I'll have a look around. Don't want to give them boys time to regroup and attack us."

"Good idea," Reese told him.

Rusty took hold of Keats and dragged the body out with him. Then he closed the door, leaving Cat and Reese alone in the room.

"Good thinking on Rusty's part, keeping an eye out," he

told her. "It would be real careless to allow Wyngate an open window and a free shot at my back."

"Look at you!" Cat cried. "You are bruises, cuts, and scrapes from one end to the other."

"Yeah," he groaned, shrugging out of the shirt. "I definitely prefer to ride on a horse, rather than follow one around on my stomach."

Cat spent a few minutes rounding up water and tearing some strips of cloth for bandages. The gunshot wound had bled some, but it had only grazed his side along his ribs.

"I spoke with a couple of the Chinese while we were getting them together," Cat said while continuing to work on his injuries. "They have been beaten and starved, and worked twelve-hour days. Dozens of them are lying in beds, sick or with broken bones." She grew very quiet. "And Rusty said he found their graveyard and counted sixty-eight markers."

Reese suffered a tightness in his chest. "Yeah, they've paid a heavy price for Wyngate's worthless tunnel. All those lives lost, and they were only about halfway through."

"From the condition of the workers, there would have been two hundred graves before they finished." She swallowed against a constriction that made her voice crack. "My Lord, Reese, two hundred lives!"

"It's over now."

"But what about Wyngate? What about the rest of the people involved?"

"We'll get them."

"Then it isn't over yet?"

"Not until someone pays the full price for those sixty-eight Chinese workers," he said, with ice lacing his words. "I'll see them behind bars or doing a jig at the end of a noose."

Rusty returned about an hour later. He was out of breath from the long night's work.

"Gone, sonny," he said. "There be nary a soul up here but us three and the Chinese. By all the saints, methinks those boys up and grew wings. It be like magic, they are all gone."

"No sign of Wyngate?"

"None."

"And the guards at the head of the trail?"

"I'm for thinking that Wyngate left so quick that they was sucked right along with him, like tumbleweeds around one of them dust devils out on the desert. We be the only ones still remaining."

"Good thing we took all of the nitro and explosives. They might have tried to block their backtrail or blown away that narrow path we have to follow out."

"'Twould appear that the Chemist and the rest were only concerned with getting away. No telling what Wyngate will do, once he feels that he is safe again."

"I'd guess his guards will head for places unknown. I don't think they'll want to listen to any more of his promises."

Rusty sighed. "Aye, you're probably right." Then he had another thought. "But what about them other two, the bandits from inside the tavern?"

"They opted not to surrender. They were in the tunnel when the powder went off."

"How considerate of them boys to save you the trouble of delivering them to the gallows."

Reese was feeling weak from loss of blood and the pounding his body had taken. He rose and put an arm around Cat for support.

"We've got a couple hundred Chinese to get back to San Francisco, Rusty. But first, we have to get word to Kim Lee right away so he and his men can put an end to the rest of this scheme. There's Judge Brown and Quan and—"

" 'Tis me that will take care of that, I reckon," he stopped Reese from continuing. "You best let the little gal put you to bed before you up and drop over."

Cat guided Reese into the bedroom and he sank down onto the bed. His head barely touched the pillow and he was sound asleep.

CHAPTER 17

IT WAS NOT quite dawn when Wyngate had shown up. Quan felt disgust, watching him grovel. The mine operator had been the man with the big plans. He had known where to find the millions in gold that would make them all rich. Now he was standing there, hat in his hand, asking for enough money to escape or hide.

"Vely hard believe," Quan finally said. "Only one marshal and alla you men run 'way?"

Wyngate twisted his hat in his hand. "He had help from an Irishman and that half-chink girl."

Quan arched his brows dramatically. "Ah yes, *big* army."

The man's face darkened. "Look, Quan, I ain't got time to stand around and talk about this. I'll get together another stake and be back. There's tons of gold up there. All I need is time to get some backers and more men. We'll be back in business in a couple months."

Quan shook his head. "I lost plenty from alla money you take."

Wyngate put his hand on his gun. "Maybe you don't understand, Quan." His voice was frigid. "I need some money, and I need it right now."

A shadow appeared from the next room. Ti Kong held his pistol ready, aimed at Wyngate's chest. The man spied him and instantly paled.

"Mabbe you big man atta Gold Spur," Quan said, smiling wide enough to show his gold teeth, "but Quan is Manchu here. You get out, never come back. Be happy Quan no kill."

Wyngate swallowed something that went down hard.

153

Quan figured it was his pride. He backed to the door, but when he opened it to leave, he froze at the entrance.

Ti Kong was close behind him. He looked out and backed up a step. There was terror in his expression when he turned to Quan and whispered, "The Kim Lee tong!"

" 'Tis speaking on behalf of Marshal Reese Corbett, the law, I am!" a powerful Irish voice resounded off of the walls. "Being too beat up to travel, he has sent me in his place. Kim Lee's men are me deputies and they surround you. Now, you men can surrender or die where you fall. It makes no difference to me what you chose."

Even as Quan tried to think of what to do, Lee's men were at the windows. He heard the crashing of glass from the back of his house. The tong members were inside his home!

Ti's panicked features were clear as he looked to Quan for instructions. Before any decision could be made, Wyngate lost his head and drew his gun. A dozen men with knives descended upon them with swift and fatal vengeance.

Cat wore an expensive hat that hid much of her face when she entered the laundry.

"Good morning," Martha Howard said anxiously. "What can I do for madam?"

"Perhaps this would be enough to take care of my account?" Cat replied.

Martha stared in wonder at the remark, as Cat removed a twenty-dollar gold piece from her lace-trimmed purse. Then she slowly raised her head so that she could look at the woman face-to-face.

Coldly, Cat said, "I believe this is the price you put on human beings, isn't it?"

Martha sucked in her breath and took an involuntary step backward. "Alley Cat!"

"Reese said he owed this to you, for telling him where I was taken that first night." She reached her hand out over the spittoon and dropped the coin into the dirty, foul liquid. Then she smiled, turned, and walked out the door, slamming it behind her.

Reese watched from the carriage as Cat exited the laundry. Her complexion was rosy and a wide smile lit up her face.

"I expect that she was somewhat surprised to see you?"

Cat giggled. "She'll probably swallow a mouthful of flies by the time she gets her mouth closed."

"You've settled your business, now I've got to finish mine."

She took a seat on the buggy next to him and regarded him with a puzzled look that knitted her brows. "But I thought you were all finished. You gave Kim Lee the deposition so he could collect the five-hundred-dollar rewards on Razor Back and the Albino Kid to cover the expense money he gave you. That makes you even with him. What else is there?"

He removed a small pouch, tossed it up, and caught it. There was the noise of coins.

"Kim Lee has a mind to be partners in a palomino ranch," Reese replied. "I didn't think you'd be happy being married to a wandering deputy marshal, so I took him up on it. Now we need to pick you up a ring and get this to the bank before the wedding."

She gasped. "The wedding!"

"Rusty is meeting us at the church, sweetheart. He's going to be best man at our ceremony—that is, if you say yes, Cathy."

Tears of happiness filled Cat's eyes. She threw her arms around Reese and said, "Yes, oh yes . . ."

The tight hug caused some discomfort from where the rope had burned about his neck, and his ribs were still tender. But it was a wonderful kind of pain. When she kissed him, he knew his search for happiness had ended. He had everything he would ever need, right there in his arms.

If you have enjoyed this book and would like to receive details on other Walker Western titles, please write to:

Western Editor
Walker and Company
720 Fifth Avenue
New York, NY 10019